SNORT OF KINGS

By

RON ELLIS

(A D.C.I. Glass crime novel)

First published in Great Britain in 1989 in Large Print by
Linford Mystery Library
F.A. Thorpe (Publishing) Ltd
Anstey, Leicestershire

This edition first published in 2007 by
Nirvana Books
Mayfiield Court Victoria Road
Freshfield Liverpool L37 7JL

10 9 8 7 6 5 4 3 2 1

ISBN 978-09549427-5-5

Printed and bound by
Beacon DM
Unit 2 Valley Road Business Park
Gas Works Road Keighley BD21 4LY

ABOUT THE AUTHOR

A former librarian, **RON ELLIS** became a DJ during Liverpool's Merseybeat era. In 1976 he was Promotions Manager for Warner Bros Records whilst he himself hit the New Wave charts in 1979 as Neville Wanker & The Punters with the self-penned 'Boys on the Dole'. In 1992, *The Sun* acclaimed him as 'The Man With The Most Jobs In Britain'.

Currently, Ron is football correspondent for the Southport Champion, runs his own publishing business and owns a property company in London's Docklands. He is also a popular after dinner speaker.

As well as the Detective-Chief Inspector Glass mysteries, Ron writes the highly-acclaimed series of crime novels set on Merseyside featuring the Liverpool DJ/Private Eye, Johnny Ace. He has published two books of poetry and is the author of the hilarious best seller, 'Journal of a Coffin Dodger', submitted for the 2004 British Comedy Awards.

2006 saw the launch of 'Southport Faces', a social history of the Lancashire town seen through the eyes of 48 local personalities and including over 200 photographs.

Ron lives on Merseyside with his wife, Sue. Their two daughters work in the fashion industry and live in Formby and Sydney respectively.

Ron's website can be found at www.ronellis.co.uk

BOOKS BY RON ELLIS

The Johnny Ace series

Ears of the city
Mean streets
Framed
The singing dead
Grave mistake
Single shot
City of vultures

The DCI Glass series

Murder first Glass
Snort of kings
Murder on the Internet

HUMOUR

Journal of a coffin dodger

POETRY

Diary of a discothèque
Last of the lake poets

HISTORY

Southport Faces

'SNORT OF KINGS'
BY
RON ELLIS

This edition is for my new, and first, grand-daughter,
Emily, and my wife, Sue, who
typed the original MSS back in the
distant days of carbon paper.

With special thanks to
Geoff Wilde for his painstaking proof reading
and David Pavitt for the typesetting

Chapter 1

The Megaphone's racing correspondent, The Hunter, was in no doubt.

'LUCK OF THE IRISH WILL WIN GOLD CUP FOR LADY VERONICA'

'I confidently predict that Tom Ball's grey mare Lady Veronica, trained in Dundalk by Eamonn Houghton, will win the Hennessy Cognac Gold Cup for Ireland at Newbury this afternoon in the face of stiff competition from the English hope, Sailor's Delight.'

Detective Chief Inspector Glass snorted over his second cup of breakfast tea in the Scotland Yard canteen.

'That should put the kiss of death on its chances,' he said, pointing out the paragraph to Sergeant Evans who was sitting beside him. 'The Hunter hasn't had a winner in three weeks.' He ate his last slice of brown toast. 'That's a hundred and eight starts you know and not a first among them.'

'Really?' Evans was impressed with his colleague's statistical knowledge. 'Perhaps he knows something nobody else does.'

'No chance. The only thing he knows is where his next drink is coming from and at the rate he's going on he won't know that soon. You know, that must be an all-time low for bad forecasting. If he can keep it up till the end of the season, he might get in the Guinness Book of Records.' He read on.

'Although the little black gelding (Sailor's Delight) carries top weight due to his tremendous

1

form last season, I cannot share the handicapper's confidence on this occasion.'

'The horse won the Cheltenham Gold Cup by a clear twenty lengths,' shouted Glass, causing others in the canteen to look up. 'What else can it do to convince him?'

'I see all the others have tipped Sailor's Delight,' observed Evans, leaning over Glass's shoulder. 'Jurex has made him his Nap of the Day.'

'And listen to this,' read Glass. 'Course Correspondent. 'I fancy Reverend Shaker to come closest to catching Sailor's Delight with perhaps the Yorkshire trained Northern Soul having the edge over Lady Veronica'. That's rubbing his nose in it.'

'So none of his colleagues agree with him?'

'Good job for them they don't or they'd all be out of a job.'

'All the same, he may know something,' said Evans stubbornly. 'I might risk 50p each way on Lady Veronica. Being a bit of a betting man, like.'

Glass shrugged his shoulders. He preferred to bet on certainties and in fact had put £5 on Sailor's Delight when the price was 3-1 instead of the current 5-4 on. 'Mainly because they named it after my cat,' he explained at the time.

'Will you be going up there this afternoon?'

Sergeant Evans shook his head. ' 'Fraid not. We've got too much on. A bank job in Putney, that stabbing in Fulham. What about you?'

'I might take a few hours off and have a look in. I haven't had a day's leave for a month.' He took a red packet from his new Harris Tweed jacket (bought at a sale in Soho, ('Closing Saturday,

2

Everything Must Go'), and extracted a cork tipped cigarette.

'Getting popular your Craven A now,' said Evans. 'You see them on all the billboards.'

'No, that's the newfangled filter tips,' said Glass. 'They've what they call 'reactivated' the brand. Ruined the buggers more like. But you can still get the old cork tips if you know where to go. Fellow in Charing Cross Road has them.' He lit up and coughed unpleasantly. 'I don't know why they can't leave things alone. There will be no traditions left for the next generation.'

'Gosh, is that the time?' exclaimed Evans, fearful of another of the Inspector's famous monologues on The Past. 'Have a good day at the races.' And he escaped through the canteen doors.

It was prophetic that Glass should go to Newbury because, over the next few weeks, he was to become very involved in the world of steeplechasing and the Hennessy Cognac Gold Cup was the start of it all.

The Hunter's real name was Elliot Guthrie. Many years ago, he had been a successful jockey but an irresistible thirst for Real Ale had swelled his stomach and unsteadied his hand until even the most experienced and good willed horses had difficulty in keeping him in the saddle.

He retired to Fleet Street where his contacts were able to secure him a post as racing correspondent on The Megaphone.

At first, he handled the job competently but, as the effects of the alcohol spread from his balance to his brain, his skills as a prophet declined.

The more he worried about the decline, the more he drank.

Eventually he was warned by his Sports Editor that if he did not improve he could go back to riding. Elliot Guthrie was now fourteen and a half stone, forty-six years old and unable to walk successfully along a straight chalk line in a police station. His prospects of a return to the turf were not good.

Guthrie knew his time was running out and he would have to start picking winners, preferably winners in big races that would be noticed. And preferably winners that other tipsters had not spotted.

The Hennessy Cognac Gold Cup would be an ideal start. He studied the formbooks, evaluated the jockeys and the trainers, weighed up the runners. The inescapable conclusion he reached was that Sailor's Delight must win. In the Cheltenham Gold Cup, run without handicaps, he had cantered home twenty lengths clear and most experts agreed that the extra weight he was carrying for the Hennessy was derisory and presented no problem to the horse.

But if, for some reason, Sailor's Delight did not finish the course . . . .

He returned to the formbooks and, after much deliberation, settled on Lady Veronica. The Irish horse had won last season's Leopardstown Chase, was good over the distance and was carrying too much weight. She must have a fair chance. He wrote his piece and handed it to the sub-editor who glanced over it with his usual expression of pity mixed with scorn.

Guthrie ignored it. He was convinced that Lady Veronica could win, if only something would happen to Sailor's Delight.

'I shan't be in tomorrow,' he told the editor. 'I am going down to Newbury for the Gold Cup.'

Dermot Draper read the morning papers with growing apprehension. Draper was a bookmaker, one of the dwindling number of one-shop owners in a profession increasingly dominated by multiples like Corals and Ladbrokes.

He had gone into bookmaking after failing his accountancy exams five years previously and, regrettably, his proficiency with figures had not improved.

Part of the fault could be attributed to sheer greed. Draper could never allow himself to lay off bets, hoping that well-backed favourites would lose and the stake money would all be his. In real life, as he found out, favourites often win.

He came from a wealthy background but his assets were now swiftly declining. He had recently taken out a second mortgage on his house, his XJ6 had been replaced by a used Ford Fiesta and, instead of her MGB, his wife was now the proud owner of a Raleigh Traveller bicycle.

His wife was far from happy with the situation being the sort of lady who preferred to live on the same exalted social plane as other bookmakers' wives. Any day now he expected her to walk out, taking the two babies with her although these would be less of a loss as they spent most of the time screaming and wetting themselves. But the alimony settlement would be high; there would be the babies' forthcoming private schooling not to mention the chiropody bills, Mrs Draper being prone to expensive diseases of the foot.

He decided to take a big gamble. His shop was in Newbury so interest in the Gold Cup was high, especially as Sailor's Delight was a local horse. He had taken over £4,000 place money on the favourite. If he stood those bets and the horse did not finish the course, that £4,000 would be his.

Dermot Draper put on his camel haired overcoat, adjusted his Robin Hood hat to a jaunty angle and, leaving the shop in the capable hands of his young assistant, set off across town for the racecourse.

The owner of Sailor's Delight spent the night before the Hennessy Cognac Gold Cup with his wife and a party of friends at the Chequers Hotel in Newbury.

Lord Crossens was forty-nine. He had inherited land from his father, the sixteenth Earl, but it was not good land. The old man had suffered from addictions to roulette, malt whisky and loose women, which had reduced his estate in Scotland from a vast forest to an orchard in twenty-three fun-packed years before his untimely demise from cardiac failure astride a Nicaraguan call-girl in Mayfair.

His eldest son, the present Earl, immediately took control of the depleted assets. He bought a bottling plant in Argyllshire and, with the aid of government grants, built up a thriving business in fruit preserves.

By the time he had reached forty, he had accumulated a small fortune, which he promptly doubled on the Stock Exchange. He also acquired a Rolls Royce, a string of racehorses and a large stomach, which was filled regularly by the top chefs in Europe.

The racehorses were his hobby. He had been able to buy from the best bloodstock in Britain, which is to say the best in the world, and his colours won the Derby and the Oaks in his first year. The other Classics quickly followed, whereupon he turned his attention to National Hunt racing.

In a short time he had added the Whitbread Gold Cup, The Massey Ferguson Gold Cup and the Cheltenham Gold Cup to his trophies.

The big one still eluded him. The Grand National.

His mare, Churchtown Jean, had fallen at Becher's when leading on the second circuit. Marmalade Soldier had only made it to the third fence when he was brought down by loose horses and the nearest he had come was when Captain Birdseye had finished seventh the previous year. On that occasion he had fired the jockey for not using his whip enough on the long run-in when the flagging beast was exhausted.

He had bought Sailor's Delight at the Doncaster Bloodstock Sales on the advice of his trainer, Albert Beaton. At first sight, the eight-year-old gelding was not an obvious champion. He had neither the grace of Arkle nor the sinewy strength of Red Rum. Furthermore, he stood only fifteen hands high, minute proportions for a steeplechaser.

'It would be like running a Chihuahua at the White City,' he said but Albert was adamant.

'I've known him since he were a two-year-old, sir. He's all right.'

'Very well, get him. But if he has not won anything in six months you're fired.'

It was no idle threat as Bertie Beaton well knew but his faith in the horse turned out to be well justified. Now his owner had his sights set on steeplechasing's richest prize.

'If Ginger McCain can do it from behind a bleddy car showroom then I'm demned sure I can.'

The Hennessy Cognac Gold Cup was the first step in the season's build-up to Aintree when Sailor's Delight would seek to be only the third horse in history to achieve the tremendous double of the Cheltenham Gold Cup and the Grand National.

Chapter 2

It was a calm December afternoon at Newbury racecourse. A pale sun warmed the air but thin columns of wood-scented smoke rising from distant chimneys suggested that evening would not be long delayed, a fact given further credence by the already lengthening shadows beneath the tall trees lining the course.

In the parade ring the stable boys were leading round the horses for the day's big race. A large crowd of serious racegoers, armed with race cards, binoculars and tattered copies of the sporting papers, studied them carefully for indications of their condition before placing last minute bets. Queues were everywhere, at the bookmakers, the Tote, the hot dog stands, the toilets and the bars. At one side of the ring owners, trainers and jockeys stood in little groups in whispered last-minute conference.

One man pushed his way through the crowds on the edge of the ring and walked past the steward into the enclosure. He wore a large, shapeless greatcoat appropriate to the season and a battered trilby hat. He made for the group of people surrounding Sailor's Delight and tapped trainer Albert Beaton on the shoulder. The trainer looked round, stared for a moment, then clasped his arms around the other's shoulders like a guest on 'This is Your Life'.

'Walter! Walter Glass! This is a surprise!' They continued to embrace, waddling in unison, their flapping coats and rocking stance giving them the appearance of copulating penguins. 'I haven't seen you for years. How are you?'

'Mustn't grumble, Bertie, mustn't grumble.'

'Still in the police?'

'Oh yes. They won't let me retire. Detective Chief Inspector now.'

'Good Lord! Should I be saluting?'

'No, but you can buy me a jar after the race.' He jerked his head towards Sailor's Delight. 'Is he going to win then?'

'He better had or I'm in trouble. Have you backed him?'

'Weeks ago when he was 3-1.'

'Not a bad price. Hey, you've not seen Nikki for a good long time.' He called over to a tall black haired girl talking to the jockey. 'She was about seven the last time, I think.' He put his arm around the girl. 'Nikki, this is an old friend of mine, Walter Glass. We did National Service together.'

'He should have been in the Cavalry, your Dad,' said Glass, admiring the girl's deep heliotrope eyes and clear skin as they shook hands. 'All he wanted to do was mess about with horses.'

'Which is why they put me in the Catering Corps. I couldn't tell one end of a joint from another.'

'Joint?' said Glass. 'I don't remember any joints. From what I remember of your cooking, Bertie, it was all porridge and stew and pretty revolting as well.'

'You were seven last time I saw Walter,' said Bertie to his daughter and to Glass, 'She's another keen on horses, just like her Dad.'

'And how's Betty?'

'Dead,' said the trainer, briefly.

'Oh, I'm sorry. I'd no idea.'

'Nor would you. No, she passed away about three years ago. Cancer.' He kept his arm round his daughter. 'I don't know where I would be without Nikki. She's a tower of strength, keeps the house going while I run the stables. And she's not a bad horsewoman either.'

'The stables doing well, are they?'

'Very well, now, Walter. Had a bit of a bad time a couple of years ago. A horse lost a race it should have won on form. There was a Stewards' Inquiry. It were favourite you see, with a lot of money on it. I were cleared, of course, but the owner took his horses away.'

'What Daddy doesn't tell you,' said Nicola, speaking for the first time, 'is that he advised the owner against running the horse because he thought it was off colour but the owner insisted and that is what happened.'

'One owner's business would not make that much difference, surely?'

'No, but racing is a funny game. They're a superstitious lot, racing folk, and if word gets around you have an unlucky yard, you can soon lose a good reputation. We had a coughing epidemic shortly after that, then a horse injured an ankle in a training gallop; both things that could happen to anybody but another owner heard the rumours and . . . ' He tailed off with a shrug.

'Well, you seem to be going all right now,' said Glass. 'I've read bits in the papers. And this fellow's got some good horses.'

'Lord Crossens? Oh aye. But he's a pain in the arse. He's only in it for the prestige and the money. Doesn't give a toss for the animals.'

Nicola interrupted. 'Excuse me but they're going out, Daddy. I want to wish Willie luck. Nice to meet you, Mr.Glass.' She ran after the horse as the entries walked down to the track.

'She's going out with Willie Leigh,' explained Bertie. 'She could do worse. He's a nice lad and well educated compared with some jockeys.'

'Look, I'd better let you get on,' said the policeman. 'I'll meet you in the Members' Bar after the last race.'

Glass went into the new stand and bought himself a cup of tea from the cafeteria on the top floor. Here he was able to catch the race through the plate glass front that offered a panoramic view of the course, sheltered from the elements. Glass took up his position on the front row of the seats.

Outside, on the rails, Elliot Guthrie alias The Hunter had moved down from his earlier spec at the parade ring.

Hovering round the bookmakers' stands on the course was bookie Dermot Draper. He, too, had watched the horses in the ring and now he was taking a last look at the prices before the race, remembering the amount he stood to 'win' if Sailor's Delight lost.

Equally apprehensive about the race was jockey Willie Leigh.

Willie had not had a good start to the season. In September his mount Golden Wonder had topped the last fence at Stratford, catapulting Willie into the path of eight pursuing horses. Luckily, he had escaped with a broken collarbone and fractured wrist but the memory of thirty-two metal clad hooves landing inches from his skull flashed into his mind at every fence he had jumped since. His nerve, if not lost, was faltering and there was extra pressure on him today, the first important race he had ridden in since the accident. He knew Lord Crossens had tried to cajole his trainer into booking another jockey, which meant he was riding for Bertie's reputation as well as his own.

All this he knew as he cantered to the start. The truth was, at twenty-nine, he was losing his passion for racing. His bones were not healing as fast as they once did and he looked to a career beyond simple riding.

They reached the start. Lord Crossens reached his box in the stand. From his seat, Glass could vaguely see the horses in the distance and wished he had brought his ex-Navy binoculars, purchased several years ago from an advert in Exchange and Mart. The starter raised his flag.

Willie licked his lips nervously but Sailor's Delight, ears pricked, black coat gleaming, was supremely oblivious to the repercussions of the result. Willie tightened his sweating hands on the reins. This was it.

'They're off.'

A roar from the crowd signalled that the Hennessy Cognac Gold Cup was under way.

The horses got off to a good start. Willie allowed his mount to run along in the centre of the pack. His main assets were his stamina plus his finishing speed, remarkable for a horse with such short legs. He preferred to let the tiring early leaders drop away after the second mile whence he would come from behind and race through the field like a two year old.

That is, if he did not fall.

Willie Leigh bit his lip nervously as they neared the first fence but the horse soared gracefully and they were over. Willie breathed again. The second obstacle was a five feet wide-open ditch in front of a four feet seven inches fence. The horse galloped strongly towards it and too late Willie tried to pull him back. They had run too close; the angle was too steep. He hung on desperately, certain they would fall, but Sailor's Delight thrust forward an extra couple of inches and, incredibly, cleared the top. He breathed again.

Watching through her glasses Nikki breathed a sigh of relief when she saw they were safely over.

The next three fences were plain and gave no trouble. At the sixth, the horse in front misjudged the downhill run, over jumped and fell but Willie managed to steer clear and as they came up to the water jump opposite the Grandstand they were lying fifth.

They swept round the left-handed course for the last time. Three horses had now either fallen or been pulled up. Reverend Shaker was leading from Boys on the Dole but Boys on the Dole was weakening. American jockey Thom Snaipe on Reverend Shaker looked round. Lady Veronica was three lengths behind and closing in. Champion jockey Charlie Higgins on the Irish horse gave her a sharp clip on her grey neck and she responded immediately, moving into second place. The fourth runner, Ankle, was tiring and Sailor's Delight moved past him and level with Boys on the Dole who looked a spent force.

In the stand Nicola Beaton clutched her programme and cheered 'Come on Willie. Come on Sailor's Delight.'

'Sailor's Delight,' roared the crowd, few of whom had not had a wager on the local favourite. Lord Crossens lit a cigar and smiled smugly. Bertie Beaton crossed his fingers, waiting for the horse to start his now famous acceleration. Dermot Draper and Elliot Guthrie were almost shaking.

Three fences to jump. Willie felt his fear drain away as he raced along in third place. Now only two fences to go and two horses to beat. He slapped Sailor's Delight on the neck. 'Come on boy, you can do it.'

Detective Chief Inspector Glass watched as, running towards him, they approached the penultimate fence. Perhaps Lady Veronica was ahead in front. 'Could The Hunter be right for once?' he thought and wished he had taken Sergeant Evans's advice and had a pound on.

But Willie Leigh knew the race was his if he just jumped the fences. Reverend Shaker was tiring fast and he knew he wouldn't last the distance. And Lady Veronica was needing too much whip.

The plain fence loomed ahead. Willie steadied himself and tightened the reins when, suddenly, the fence seemed to move. He blinked. A split second later he felt himself falling.

The horse hesitated; not knowing why his rider had pulled back but it was too late for him to stop so he gave a tremendous leap to clear the fence.

Willie was not with him. He lay in a crumpled heap on the ground as Sailor's Delight raced instinctively after the other horses.

By good fortune he lay so close to the fence that the horses following did not touch him. The course ambulance roared up the track as the crowd kept their eyes on the leaders.

Charlie Higgins had the race sewn up. Whip still swinging, he galloped past the post on Lady Veronica a good length clear of Reverend Shaker with the Yorkshire bay, Northern Soul, coming in third after a good late run.

Bertie Beaton ran onto the course to retrieve his horse which had pulled up of his own accord some way past the finishing post. Nicola ran towards the fence where Willie lay unconscious, in time to go with him to hospital.

Lord Crossens spat the end of his cigar to the ground, cursing the name of Willie Leigh. 'The incompetent bungler never rides for me again. Letting a little horse like that throw him. The beggar is hardly more than a bleddy pony.'

Dermot Draper and Elliot Guthrie left the course rejoicing in their good fortune.

Popular opinion was that Willie had been thrown or, at best, fallen off. Glass, without the benefit of his ex-Navy binoculars, could not tell either way.

But Willie Leigh, lying in the ambulance, was quite certain. He had not been thrown, neither had he fallen. He could remember quite clearly that last jump.

And he knew he had been unconscious BEFORE he hit the ground.

Chapter 3

'Are you sure?' asked Nicola Beaton. It was the day after the race and Willie, released from hospital after overnight observation, had taken her to dinner at a country restaurant near Oxford, not far from her father's stables, a half-timbered building that had once been a barn.

'Positive,' he said, taking a mouthful of homemade leek soup.

'What does it mean?'

'I don't know but one thing is certain. I have never had a blackout before, not even after concussion.'

'Did the specialist say it was concussion?'

'The specialist did not know. He checked me over, took my blood pressure, listened to my heart, X-rayed my bones and, apart from the broken ribs and collar-bone, said there was nothing wrong.'

He paused as a waitress in a gingham dress took away the soup dishes.

'So what do you think happened?'

'Well, you don't knock yourself out falling on your chest so I think someone had a go at me.'

'But how? There was hardly anyone at that part of the course and what could they have done? Blown a poisoned dart at you?'

Willie weighed his words carefully. 'I think I was drugged, probably between the second race and the Hennessy. Easy enough to do. Something in my tea, jab of a needle in the crowd.' The wine waiter came forward with a bottle of Liebfraumilch, which Willie dutifully tasted and approved.

'But, if what you say is true, who could it be and why?'

'Anybody's guess. Perhaps someone had it in for me. Or for the owner or even your father.'

'Oh no.'

'Don't worry. It's far more likely they just wanted Sailor's Delight to lose and thought it easier to get at me than the horse.'

Proving it was another thing. Willie spoke to nobody else about his suspicions thinking, probably correctly, that they would merely dismiss them as excuses.

Bertie Beaton, being a kind man, said nothing and did not cancel any of Willie's rides although Lord Crossens insisted that other jockeys be brought in to ride his horses.

'That, of course, is your privilege,' said Bertie and to Willie he said 'Don't let it worry you. I will have plenty of other rides to keep you going when you get back.'

But Willie was not anxious to race again in a hurry. Normally a broken collar-bone and ribs would keep a jockey out of the saddle for little more than a fortnight or three weeks. Bertie feared that the jockey might be losing his confidence, indeed he privately thought that he must have made a mistake on Sailor's Delight.

Nicola was frightened that if someone was after her boyfriend they might try something else. 'We can only wait and see,' said Willie but Nicola Beaton was not a girl for waiting.

By chance, Detective Chief Inspector Glass was at his desk at Scotland Yard when the telephone call came. He could hear the instrument ringing although it took him some moments to locate it beneath the mountains of paper on his desk.

He barked angrily into the mouthpiece. 'Glass.'

'Oh Mr.Glass. This is Nicola Beaton. You remember we met at Newbury last week when you were talking to my father in the parade ring.'

'Nikki, of course. How is your boyfriend? The papers say he's recovering but that can mean anything.'

'He's getting better but still feeling rather shaken and, of course, he'll not be able to ride again until his collar-bone is mended.' She didn't add that he was currently too terrified to mount even a Shetland pony. 'Er, actually, it was about Willie that I was ringing, about the race, that is.'

Glass sat up a little straighter. He recognised a tone in her voice that told him he was about to hear something important. It was a tone informers often used when they had information to impart and Glass set great store by informers.

'Why don't you come and see me? Can you get up to London?'

'I'm in London now. I'm staying here for a couple of days with some friends.'

Glass glanced at his ex-Navy chronograph. 'Well it's eleven thirty now, no hang on, that's in Buenos Aires, it's half past five here. Look, I'm going to my daughter's for dinner this evening. Why don't you come along and join us? You can get to Wimbledon, can you? They live just by the Common.'

'I have my car but listen, your daughter won't want me coming along at the last minute, just like that.'

'Nonsense,' said Glass who could always be relied upon to misjudge a woman's reactions.

'You're about the same age, you'll get on well. Shall we say about seven, give you plenty of time to fight your way through the rush hour traffic?'

'All right. If you're sure?'

'Of course.' He gave her the address. 'I'll be there myself by then anyway.' Punctuality was never one of his strong points.

'Sorry I'm late,' said Glass, struggling to extricate himself from the rain-sodden greatcoat. 'Traffic, you know, on Waterloo Bridge.'

'There usually is,' agreed his daughter.

Glass ignored the remark. 'I hope the dinner isn't ruined.'

'Ours isn't,' said Sue. 'We've eaten it. I believe you've met Nikki?'

'Er yes.' The detective was no match for the modern young woman.

'Something came up at the Yard. That's why I'm late.'

'In the bar probably.'

'Anyway I see your husband isn't here yet.'

'He's out on a case.'

'Ah, that's what all policemen say,' leered Glass maliciously.

'Can you think of anything worse?' Sue said to Nikki. 'A father and a husband, both policemen.'

'A trainer and a jockey come close,' replied Nikki, and you get the smell of manure as an added bonus.'

'Yes, at least my men don't smell.' Sue eyed Glass surreptitiously lighting a Craven A. 'Except of tobacco. I'll get your dinner. It's dried stew.'

'Just like your father used to make in the cookhouse,' smiled the policeman to Nicola. The front door opened and a tall blond man in his late thirties walked into the room.

'Good timing Robin. The stew has dried to a tee. Nikki, this is my son-in-law, Robin Knox, Detective Chief Inspector as he is known to the underworld. Nicola Beaton, daughter of an old friend of mine, Bertie Beaton.'

'Not the racing trainer?' smiled Knox, taking her hand.

'Another betting man?' she smiled back.

'Only the Derby and the National. But I like to go to the odd meeting.'

'He means Ascot,' said Glass, 'where he can wear his top hat.'

'Ah, a social race goer.'

Sue came in, kissed her husband and put a plateful of brown congealed matter in front of him, similar to the brown congealed substance on Glass's plate. 'I couldn't help it,' she said defensively. 'You were late.'

'I was on a case.'

'That's what all policemen say. Anyway, it is very good for you, all vegetables, celery, mushrooms and things. They tend to dry after a while, that's all.'

'They do?' queried Glass, whose top dentures were fighting a losing battle with dried potato and were in imminent danger of joining the rest of his dinner on the plate.

'If you can't eat it, give it to Tinker.'

'God, your cat would eat anything. With Sailor it's fresh fish or nothing.' He spat the potato out. 'What case have you been on?' he asked Robin Knox.

'Missing body,' said Knox briefly, always reluctant to discuss his cases.

'Missing from where?'

'Missing from the head,' said Knox. 'We found that in Covent Garden tube station this morning. Is there any tea?'

Glass turned to Nicola. 'Do you want to tell me about Willie? You need not worry about Sue and Robin.' He did not share his son-in-law's reticence. It was feared at the Yard that Glass would discuss important cases with strangers on trains, just to while away the journey.

'Finish your meal first,' ordered Sue. 'Then she can tell you over coffee in the lounge.'

An hour later they were enjoying Cona coffee with cream, apart from Glass who preferred tea, and Nicola had finished expounding Willie's theories about his fall.

'Don't they give jockeys blood tests if they think they have been doped?' asked Glass, dipping a chocolate Home Wheat biscuit in his tea.

'Nobody thought he had. It looked like an accident.'

'And he never told them anything different?'

'It would have looked like he was making excuses.'

'He could be right.'

'And the hospital was more concerned with his broken bones.'

'Was the horse dope tested?'

'As a matter of fact, yes. They do random tests as well as checking the first three. But Sailor's Delight's test was negative.'

'Which means we have nothing at all to go on apart from your boyfriend's suspicions and he could be mistaken or covering up.'

Nicola reddened. 'I assure you that he is neither.'

'Well let us believe he is right. The obvious favourite must be some sort of racing coup, to prevent the horse from winning. Somebody with money on it to lose.'

'Or somebody who didn't like Willie?'

'Easier to hit him on the head on a dark night,' said Glass. 'What is this owner chap like?'

'Lord Crossens? Large, self opinionated and a millionaire.'

'He'll have made a few enemies then, if only through envy. But, again, why not just run him over, why all this? No, it's got to be a profit motive.'

'So what can you do?'

'Absolutely nothing,' said Glass. 'But you can. Keep your eyes open and ring me the minute anything at all suspicious happens.'

'In other words,' said Knox, 'join the unpaid millions working for Scotland Yard through the courtesy of Chief Inspector Glass.'

'Nothing wrong in that either. Without members of the public coming forward our success rate would be halved overnight.'

'I will do that,' said Nicola. 'Thanks for listening anyway. And I will ring you if anything happens.'

She did ring again but not until Christmas and, at Christmas, Robin Knox was busy escorting a black pop star round the country.

Chapter 4

The Assistant Commissioner had called the top-level conference to which Detective Chief Inspector Robin Knox had been summoned. Also present were Superintendent Cecil Page of the Drugs Squad and a tall, trendily dressed man in his late forties who was introduced to Knox as the president of a multi-national record company.

'We have known for some time,' opened the Assistant Commissioner, 'that the market for cocaine in this country is controlled by one big buyer. Very simply, we want to know who he is.'

'I have authorised you, Chief Inspector, to be seconded to the Drugs Squad for an indefinite period of time.'

'The point is,' said Superintendent Page in soft Birmingham tones, 'you are a new face. Many of our lads are known to people in this business.'

'And it is a business too,' said the A.C. 'Cocaine has overtaken heroin as the most popular hard drug. It is now a growth industry worth several million pounds a year. Tax free.'

'How does Mr. Vaughan here fit in?' asked Robin, indicating the record company president.

'In one week's time an American pop singer called Shula Sun is coming to Britain for a nine day promotion tour. She will be visiting local radio and TV stations and, at night, making personal appearances in discotheques and dance halls. Sun is a known cocaine addict.'

'So are many pop stars, especially American ones.'

'I see you have a knowledge of the industry,' commented the other drily.

'Well, Sun and her entourage will be searched thoroughly at Heathrow to make sure they do not bring any of the stuff with them, thus making it certain they will try to obtain some while they are here. In fact, they will probably not be all that secretive about it as sniffing is a common habit in their circles. Once contact is made with a pusher, your job will be to follow that lead until you get to the top man.'

'But how do I get to meet Shula Sun?'

The record company chief spoke up. 'You've been appointed manager on the tour. Luckily, most record companies bring in independent firms to help with promotion and publicity so it will not be thought strange. You'll be travelling with Miss Sun and her manager, driving them to each town, making sure they get to the hotels etc.'

'What about the visits?'

'Don't worry about those. Our regional promotion men will take care of those. They will meet you at the hotels each morning, take Shula and her manager to the radio stations and bring them back to you in time to go round the discotheques at night.'

'I go with them to the clubs then do I?'

'Yes. Three places each night. She'll go on stage, mime to the record, sign a few photographs; all the publicity is organised.'

'You're virtually just the driver,' said Superintendent Page.

'Should we have heard of this Shula Sun?' asked the Assistant Commissioner.

'She's had a couple of hit records in the States. Now we're trying to break her over here. We're giving away 10,000 vouchers offering 50p off the record but only exchangeable at chart return shops. This should get the record into the Top 75 whereupon we can get on 'Top of the Pops' which means an extra 20,000 sales straight away.'

'This smacks of Payola.'

'Quite legal I assure you,' said Vaughan.

'Is this tour a put-up job to get at this organisation?'

'Oh no, Robin. Scotland Yard have been considering for a long time how to break this ring from the inside. The show business route seemed the best way and, as I already knew Mr Vaughan here and knew he felt as strongly as we do about the evils of drug trafficking, I got in touch with him. As the boss of an international record company with strong American connections, he seemed the ideal person to help us. I might add that nobody from his company knows about this and you yourself will be known as Jeremy Rowlands of Ra Ra Promotions.'

'Here is your itinerary.' Vaughan handed the detective a fourteen-page booklet. 'All the hotels are down here, the names of the club managers and disc jockeys. I suggest you phone each one the day before to confirm your visit. We have another, 'genuine', publicity company going round ahead of you doing the displays and arranging press advertising.'

'Very efficient,' said Knox. 'I hope the record sells.'

'The Americans will be very upset if it doesn't. Do you like pop music yourself, Chief Inspector?'

'I'm more into Simon and Garfunkel,' said Knox.

'Just one thing, whatever you do, don't let Shula Sun near a microphone.'

'But I thought she was singing along to the record in the clubs.'

'Miming along to be exact. You see, it's impossible to recreate the sound on record which took hours of electronic manipulating to achieve.'

'You mean she can't sing?'

'I mean it's better if she doesn't try.'

'Who do I report to?' Knox asked the Assistant Commissioner.

'We thought you could get in touch with your own sergeant, Evans isn't it? Far too risky to contact Superintendent Page. Ring Evans at home and remember you are Jeremy Rowlands at all times. Evans will be known as Arthur Meadowcroft, a friend of yours who is in the graphic design business and has drawn a few album covers for you.'

Knox could imagine nobody less like a graphic designer than Sergeant Evans whose prints of 'The Green Lady' and 'The Hay Wain' made his living room a replica of a million suburban lounges up and down the country.

'I wouldn't advise cutting your hair any shorter,' added Vaughan. 'Only young trendies and new skinheads wear it short. We ageing record executives keep it long to remind us of our hippie days.'

'So that's about it, Robin,' said the Assistant Commissioner. 'The tour starts on the fifteenth. You know what we are after. I'll want results.'

Detective Chief Inspector Glass was at his daughter's when Knox came home with the news of his assignment.

'Spending a week away with a black woman, eh? That's the sort of thing that makes these modern marriages so successful.'

'I trust him implicitly,' said Sue, 'and nobody asked your opinion.'

'I prefer Vera Lynn to all these blues people,' remarked Glass who had little knowledge of popular music, his interest being confined to the slow foxtrot at the Compton Road Welfare and Social Club. 'Her and P.J.Proby.'

'So long as he brings me an expensive present to make up for all the steaks and champagne I'll be missing.'

They all treated it light-heartedly but Robin Knox knew this was a dangerous job. If his cover were blown he could expect no mercy.

And his forebodings were to be proved right.

Chapter 5

Detective Chief Inspector Robin Knox, alias Jeremy Rowlands, waited at Heathrow Air Terminal for his pop star to disembark. He wore a sweat shirt bearing the logo 'Trolfid Records', a pair of tight brown cords and a coney fur jacket to keep off the chill December wind. He looked every inch a record promoter.

Shula Sun was equally recognisable as 'showbiz' when she pirouetted through the barrier resplendent in full-length white mink coat, accompanied by a short man wearing a Texas cowboy hat and ski boots. She stood almost six feet tall and wore a bright red frizzy wig which, against her black skin and white coat, gave her the appearance of a flag.

Knox went across to introduce himself. 'Jeremy Rowlands.'

'Hi man, I'm Frankie Lucerelli, Shula's road manager. Wow, this is some weather, man! Do you know it is eighty-one degrees in Florida?'

'You've come from there?'

'Miami.' He spoke with a Bronx accent with undertones of his Italian ancestry. Beneath the hat greasy black hair splayed to his shoulders and a thin covering of similar hair masked his face. Passing strangers might have mistaken him for a Mexican bandit.

'The car's outside,' said Knox. 'I'll give you a hand with the luggage.' There were five large cases.

'Shula's dresses,' said Lucerelli, allowing Knox to carry the three heaviest.

Knox led the way to the Toyota Crown saloon hired for the tour. 'We've just got time to change and have a meal at the hotel before we go to the first club.'

'Oh man, I don't wanna go to no club tonight. I'm beat.' The singer spoke for the first time, her only previous acknowledgement of her new acquaintance being an amused smile as she watched him struggle with her luggage.

'But it's on the itinerary.'

'I don't give a damn about the itinerary. I ain't goin' to no club tonight, right?'

Lucerelli patted Knox's arm. 'Don't worry, man. I can handle her. You just get us to that hotel.'

They were booked into Whites in Bayswater Road. A blue uniformed porter assisted with the luggage. In the foyer a group of women from the record company were waiting to organise various aspects of publicity for the tour, press hand-outs, photos, press conference dates and vouchers. They were hoping that Miss Sun would discuss these things with them but she flounced up to the suite reserved for the party and it was left to Lucerelli to deal with them. He led them into the bar.

Knox went up to his own bedroom, ran a hot bath to which he added the tube of French herb foam provided and spent a luxurious half hour beneath the steaming water. By the time he returned to the hotel bar, newly changed into clean denims and Ra Ra Publicity T-shirt, the singer and her manager were on their third whisky.

'It's okay, man,' Lucerelli reassured him. 'Shula is set to go, ain't you baby?' The superstar gave a big white smile.

'You sorted out the girls?' asked Knox.

'Yeah, no problem and they sorted me out too.' He took from his pocket a substance not unlike tobacco. 'I've been beating my brains out for some grass and here we are.' Chuckling to himself, he produced a rolling machine and some papers and proceeded to make a cigarette.

'You want one?' he offered generously but Knox declined.

The first venue that evening was a dance hall in North London. Both passengers smoked steadily throughout the journey so that the air inside the car was redolent with the sweet smell of marijuana. For her first stage appearance, Shula Sun wore a backless, almost frontless sequinned dress which was of little benefit to her as she had the bust of a sixteen year old boy. Lucerelli still sported his Texas hat like an extra from 'Dallas'.

Outside the dance hall were displayed posters advertising the visit and a few kids hung around the entrance, not so much in wait for Shula Sun but rather because they could not afford the entrance fee.

In the foyer the manager in bow tie and black suit greeted them effusively, kissing Shula Sun on both cheeks before leading them to his office.

'Shula will mime to the record,' explained Knox, 'and sign a few photographs. The whole thing can be over in twenty minutes.'

'Oh no, you must stay and have a meal with us and I'll open a few bottles of the house bubbly.'

'Suits me,' said Lucerelli who had eaten the four-course hotel dinner barely an hour before. 'I could murder a steak.'

'We have the 12 inch record all ready.'

'Oh, I'm afraid she only sings to the 7 inch,' said Knox hurriedly. 'This one goes on all night, the 12 inch. We would need sleeping bags.' Forced laughter filled the tatty room. 'And about fifty photos should be enough.'

'You're joking. There are over five hundred kids out there. You will need a couple of hundred at least.'

'We'd better get her to start signing them in the car for tomorrow night then,' Knox murmured to Lucerelli.

They went out into the ballroom. The noise, emanating from eight speaker bins placed strategically round the dance floor, was deafening and the multicoloured flashing lights and laser beams reflecting off the mirror ball gave Knox an instant headache. He preferred the more subtle sophistication of Tramps. On the floor itself the kids, between eleven and sixteen, danced in frenzied confusion.

'And now folks, I think she is here at last.' The resident DJ, who could have been earning more money as a gravedigger, brought the audience to a peak of excitement as he introduced Shula. She walked on confidently wearing her chin-splitting smile and mimed in almost perfect time to her record. Then Lucerelli and Knox threw unsigned photographs and '50p Off' vouchers into the air and watched the kids fight like animals to catch them as they fluttered to the ground.

'They'll all be in the litter bin by midnight,' commented a nearby doorman who had seen it all before.

Knox slipped away to the foyer to ring Sergeant Evans from the public pay phone. 'Jeremy Rowlands here,' he announced.

'Oh hello, sir. How's it going? Enjoying the high life?'

'She's a pain in the backside but things are happening. Her manager got hold of some cannabis within five minutes of reaching the hotel.'

'A contact from the States do you think?'

'No, some women from the record company but it's my bet he's asked them to fix him up with some cocaine which, as most of the people in this business seem to be on one thing or another, they'll probably be able to do without difficulty. I'm just waiting to see who comes along.'

At that moment Knox saw Lucerelli coming along towards his phone box.

'...so if you can get some rough sketches down, Art, I'll call in and see them when I get back to town.'

'Somebody's come, have they sir?' said Evans with lightning insight. 'I'll be getting back to the wife then.'

'Be lucky,' he turned to the American. 'Just fixing up some album covers. How's it going?'

'The steaks are ready.'

'I meant the performance.'

'Oh that's fine. She'll be signing that lot for a good quarter hour. We can be getting on with eating and drinking.'

'Had you met Shula before this trip?' asked Knox as they walked to the restaurant where the manager was waiting for them, bottles uncorked.

'Hell, no. And I don't wanna meet her again after this. Man, she thinks she is a superstar and what is she? Just a two bit kid from Georgia who hit it lucky with a couple of records.'

'So who do you work for?'

'I work for me, baby. I just hire myself out to any company wanting to put a tour on the road.

Normally I do bands and concerts, not PR jobs like these but, I'd never been to England, the job came up and I thought, what the hell; another part of the world I can see for nothing.' He looked at Knox's plate. 'You don't seem to be too hungry there. Do you want me to take one of those steaks off your hands?' His fork reached across. 'May as well eat it while it's there. You never know when the next one is coming.'

He'd got through a full bottle of imitation champagne by the time Shula came off stage, breathless and excited by her reception.

'Don't get too happy, Baby, they would scream for the janitor if he got up on that rostrum.'

The second venue of the evening was a gay club in the West End. They arrived about midnight to find over a thousand people crammed into a vast cellar. All male. Young, soft-skinned waiters dressed in tight satin shorts with cutaway inside legs and matching vests, padded gently round the edge of the packed dance floor. It was so hot that recycled sweat dripped from the low ceiling as rain.

The manager was very proud of his club. 'All the trends start here, love,' he said to Knox. 'Dancing, fashion, records, we are six months ahead of anybody in town.'

'Yeah, it's the same in the States,' said Lucerelli. 'All the discos pick up the scene from the gays.'

'I go down a bomb in gay clubs,' said Shula. 'This is really where my head is at.'

She proceeded to prove it. Her record brought roars of approval, she was mobbed for photographs; it took an hour to get her away.

'Funny,' said Knox. 'You wouldn't think they'd like a woman singer, especially dressed or undressed like she is.'

'Oh no. They love the glamour because half of them would like to dress like that themselves. And, of course, her music over here is ahead of its time. When she starts having hits they'll move on to something new.' Lucerelli was obviously well up in the philosophy of the pop scene.

At the hotel, he suggested more drinks and some supper. Shula declined but Knox joined him in the bar. He wanted more information about the drugs.

'I could have had her tonight,' he remarked casually as he bit into a giant beef sandwich. 'She asked me but I said 'no'. Does 'em good to keep them waiting. I might have her tomorrow when she is desperate. Do you fancy a go?'

'No thank you,' said Knox politely. 'Do you think you're going to enjoy the tour?'

'Now that I got some grass I am and tomorrow those girls have fixed it up with some guy to bring down some coke.'

Knox was excited. The contact had come sooner than he expected. 'But we're in Nottingham tomorrow.'

'That's right. Is that far from London?'

'About a hundred miles, maybe more.'

'Is that all?' Lucerelli was an experienced Greyhound traveller. Anything under a thousand miles to him was a mere bus stop away.

'Where are you meeting him?'

'He's coming to the hotel. It is the Albany, isn't it?' Knox nodded. 'Some time around tea time, when we get back from the radio stations.'

'Ah.' Knox nodded again.

'So if you want any, he can fix you up.' The American finished the last giant beef sandwich, leaned back in his chair and scratched his hair under the hat. 'Say, what are these radio stations like over here? Beacon is it we're going to and Trent?'

'I don't know,' said Knox guardedly, having never been inside a local radio station in his life. 'The regional guy from Trolfid is meeting us in the Albany at lunchtime and he'll be taking you up to Trent and, I think, Radio Derby.'

'So what time do we have to leave?'

'We have to be in Nottingham for twelve so nine thirty I think.'

'Jeez, and it's nearly three now. I'm gonna grab me some sleep. It takes me an hour to wake her in the mornings. I think I'll book her an alarm call for six, that will get her up.'

Knox decided against ringing Evans at three in the morning to impart the latest move. It was also a little late to ring Sue. But it was working all according to plan. The next day he would take the first step on the trail of Mr.Big.

Chapter 6

Lucerelli ate a hearty grilled breakfast. Shula Sun managed a weak coffee, complaining that someone had called her up at six in the morning. As it was, she staggered down to the restaurant at nine fifteen. Knox had paid the bill by then and was ready to leave. He was not sure how the record company would react when they received the account. Two hundred and thirty-eight pounds for three people for one night seemed excessive. He wondered if they would charge Lucerelli for the four phone calls to America and the six double whiskies.

They set off on time, Lucerelli still wearing his hat, Shula Sun back with the mink but with a purple wig and Knox in a black bomber jacket and cords. More doped cigarettes were smoked on the journey and, having ascertained that Shula Sun disliked rock'n'roll, Lucerelli played Chuck Berry cassettes all the way up the M1.

The Trolfid regional promotion man, Sandy Heneghan, was waiting for them at the Albany. 'I'm glad you got here,' he said when the introductions had been effected. 'I told Trent we would be in the studio for twelve.'

'You two go with him in his car,' instructed Knox. 'You can leave me to take the cases in.'

'I want some dresses out first,' said the singer.

'Christ Almighty, it's bloody radio, who's gonna see you?'

'I'll put Shula's cases in my boot,' said Sandy Heneghan hurriedly, anxious to avoid any hassle. At twenty-four, he already had the promotion man's standard worried expression. The swollen purple veined nose and nervous tics would come later.

'Fine. I'll see you back at the hotel at six then.'

Knox had lunch in the hotel then retired to his room to phone his wife. She wanted to discuss the arrangements for Christmas ('You know my father is staying for the week'). He did not mind. He quite enjoyed Glass's company. He also rang Sergeant Evans to inform him of the forthcoming meeting with Mr.Big.

'Is that what they call him?' asked Evans.

'It's what I call him. It sounds suitably melodramatic as befits this case.' He described Shula Sun's outfit, the gay club and the champagne. 'And her manager is straight out of the Mafia.'

'Just up your street I'd say. Back to the playboy life for you.'

'You know perfectly well I'm a respectable married man now, Sergeant, just like yourself. Or would you like me to fix you up for a week with Shula Sun?'

'I don't think Mrs.Evans would approve,' chortled the sergeant.

'I'll be in touch when I have some news, probably tomorrow.' Knox smiled into the phone. 'Bye, Art.'

He took the lift down to the hotel lobby and asked the receptionist if there was anything on in Nottingham that afternoon.

'Just the same as any other afternoon in Nottingham,' she replied. 'Nothing to do except the pictures.'

'Isn't there racing on today?' said her companion. 'I'm sure I read it in the paper this morning.'

There was. 'Could you ring me a taxi?' he asked. 'It may not be Ascot but it will be better than being chatted up in dark cinemas by old ladies with wet umbrellas and packets of Mintoes.'

The Nottingham racecourse was on the Colwick Road, only a ten minute drive from the hotel. He was in time to see the second race but the names of the horses meant nothing to him. The fresh air, however, was a welcome contrast to the mephitic atmosphere of the previous night's club. He went across to the parade ring to watch the runners come out for the next race.

'I didn't think social racegoers came to Nottingham,' said a voice beside him. He turned to see a tall, black haired girl.

'Hello,' he said in some surprise. 'It's Nikki Beaton isn't it? Have you got horses racing here today?'

'Only one, in the next race. The chestnut over there, number six.'

'Will it win?'

'I hope so. You can have a bet if you like. It's called Killarney Heights.'

'Is your boyfriend riding it?'

'No, Willie isn't riding yet. It's only three weeks since his accident. Give him a chance.'

'Did anything more come of that, the - er trouble I mean?'

'Nothing at all. But I still believe Willie,' she added defiantly.

'Well, if somebody did try to stop Sailor's Delight winning they succeeded and probably made a lot of money which means they will almost certainly repeat the operation. Thieves are greedy.'

Nikki pursed her lips thoughtfully. 'You haven't met my father have you? Come over and say hello, he would like to meet you.'

Bertie Beaton was assisting the jockey onto Killarney Heights. He and Knox shook hands and chatted for a few minutes, mainly about their common acquaintance, Detective Chief Inspector Glass.

'Are you in Nottingham on a case?' asked Nikki, 'or just on holiday?'

'Oh no, I'm working.'

'You don't look very much like a detective today,' she said, eyeing his leather jacket and jeans. 'Nor a social racegoer.'

Knox smiled disarmingly. 'I'm in disguise.'

She looked at him quickly. 'You're not here because of . . .'

'No, I promise you. I had a free afternoon and thought I would come to the races, there being little else to do in Nottingham. Meeting you here was a pure coincidence and a delightful one too.'

He stayed with them for the race, which Killarney Heights won by four lengths. Afterwards they had a celebratory drink before Knox had to leave for the Albany. 'Don't forget,' he said, repeating Glass's words, 'if you do see anything suspicious, ring us.'

He was back at the Albany Hotel in time for his party's return. They arrived at five, Shula in a rage because they had cut short her interview and Heneghan suitably cringing and apologetic. Lucerelli seemed quite unconcerned. Knox was not sure whether to stick by the manager until the contact showed up or hope Lucerelli would invite him along. The decision was made for him.

'I'm going up to my room,' said the American. 'I'll see all you guys later.'

'We have to be in Derby for eight. Do you want dinner before we go?'

'Oh sure, I'll only be an hour or so. We can eat at six thirty.'

Lucerelli's room was on the same corridor as his, two doors along. Shula Sun slept between them. Knox waited until they had gone upstairs in the lift before following. He stepped out cautiously at the sixth floor. There was no sign of them. Both bedroom doors were shut. He decided to stay by the lift doors so that if they came out unexpectedly they would think he was waiting for the lift. This way he would see all visitors.

Five minutes passed then the lift drew up to his floor, the bell tinkled and the gates opened to reveal an elderly man in an expensive suit who took the opposite corridor to his room. Knox pretended to be shining his shoes on the automatic machine.

Half an hour later he was still shining his shoes as various guests arrived and departed. Nobody went near the rooms of Shula Sun or her manager. He rubbed the stray polish from the hem of his jeans.

When the lift came up yet again, Knox knew immediately that it held the man he was waiting for. He looked like a throwback to Woodstock with straw coloured, shoulder length hair, dark glasses and faded denims; he was carrying a brown attaché case.

Knox shone his shoes for a final time as he watched the man go to Lucerelli's door and tap three times. He allowed him three minutes after he had gone in then sauntered up himself and knocked hard.

'Who is it?' called an American voice.

'Jes.' Knox could not bring himself to use the name Jeremy.

'Hang on.' Footsteps, then the bolt went back and the door opened. The policeman looked in surprise. On the writing table was set up a pair of gold miniature scales. In the left hand pan were tiny matching weights and in the right hand pan....a quantity of fine white powder, barely enough to cover a ten pence piece.

'You managed to get some then?' said Knox nonchalantly. He walked in.

'And the very best too. Three hundred dollars for this. Hey, I forgot, do you still want some, man?'

'There's none left,' said the vendor quickly. 'Your singer had five hundred dollars of it. This is the last.'

Knox smiled benevolently and closed the door behind him. 'Can you get any more?'

'Sure he can, man. I tell you, this little lot ain't gonna last me the whole tour.'

The man finished weighing the powder and poured it carefully into a small silver container that he handed to Lucerelli. 'I guess so,' he said, 'but it might take a week.'

'Hell, we go back to the States on the 23rd, that's a week today.'

'I don't,' said Knox quickly.

'Who is this guy?' the stranger asked Lucerelli.

'Jeremy Rowlands,' said Knox, 'Who are you?'

'This is Richard,' Lucerelli said. Knox moved forward to shake hands but Richard just nodded. 'Our tour manager,' added the American.

'You don't work for the record company.'

So he must be pretty well in with the people there, thought Knox. 'No, I work for myself, Ra Ra

Promotions,' he said. 'The record company hired me for this tour, which means I can arrange to see you anytime.'

'You're based in London then?'

'Yes, but I travel around all the time.'

'Where do you usually buy your coke?'

'Different places, wherever it comes. As I said, I travel a lot.' He decided to try flattery. 'But it's not often as good as this. If you can get more of this quality you might have got yourself a regular customer.'

'We shall see about that,' said Richard dubiously. To Lucerelli: 'Is he OK?'

'Christ, man. Jes is an old friend. What's with all the stalling? Any buddy of mine is OK.'

'You just can't be too careful. Nobody is what they seem these days.'

You can say that again, thought Knox.

'Can you get to Birmingham on the 26th?'

'That's Boxing Day.'

'Right. I'm on the show at the Odeon that night.'

'Richard is a roadie,' explained Lucerelli in reply to Knox's raised eyebrows.

'Do you mind? Lighting engineer,' said Richard in a haughty tone.

Knox tried to place the accent but without success. His words were well modulated, he was obviously well educated, even cultured, but the detective could not pin him down to a specific part of the country.

'Boxing Day will be fine,' he said. 'Where and when?'

'Book into the Albany Hotel. I'll be there between five and seven. I'll come up to your room. And remember, I'll want pound notes.'

Lucerelli took the cue and handed across eight crisp twenty-pound notes. 'You wanna sniff?' he asked Knox, holding out the silver box.

'No thanks. Not before dinner. After the show. Listen, I'm going to get Shula organised or we won't have time to eat. We have to be in Derby in an hour and a half.'

'Always time to eat, man,' said Lucerelli who had sampled the canteens of three radio stations during the afternoon. Knox observed that his stomach, which protruded at intervals through his shirt, was covered with the same matted black hair as his face and head.

Richard folded up his scales and put them into his attaché case. 'A pleasure to do business with you,' he said, politely. 'I'll see you,' he told Knox, 'on the 26th.'

'I'll be there.'

Lucerelli roused his singer by beating several times on the wall with an Indian club ('a mascot from L.A.' he told Knox) and they all went down to dinner in the Four Seasons Restaurant. Knox had the duckling.

The first gig was at a dance hall in Derby where the surroundings and the audience were identical to the North London venue the night before.

'Very young audiences at dance halls these days,' commented Knox to the manager.

'It's the 9-15 year olds that buy the records,' he replied. 'While they are still at school. Once they start work they can't afford it, not at over a pound for a single.'

The DJ organised silly competitions which Shula was asked to judge. He made some hapless competitors drink a pint of shandy then swallow a raw egg ('First to finish wins a T shirt'). Others had to remove intimate items of their clothing and carry them to the stage. The sight of pre-pubescent schoolgirls waving their training bras in the air was too much for Lucerelli.

'I just gotta get hold of a woman tonight,' he said, his eyes glazed with naked lust. 'What's this place like we're going to next because this here is just jailbait, man.'

It was a nightclub in Nottingham and when they arrived, it was deserted.

'Nobody comes in until after eleven, when the pubs are shut', explained the manager. 'But don't worry, I have a meal and some champagne ready for you in the bistro.'

Knox was about to protest they had had dinner when Lucerelli dug him in the ribs. 'I'll eat yours if you ain't hungry, no sweat.'

'You can eat mine too,' offered Shula Sun in a rare burst of speech. For practically the entire trip Knox had barely heard her speak except when microphones were thrust into her face, whereupon she became garrulous. 'I don't know why they don't have proper food in this country.' She turned angrily on Knox. 'Where can you get grits and black-eyed peas?'

'Sooooul food,' sang Lucerelli, rolling his eyes to Heaven like a demented Al Jolson.

'We have Bird's Eye peas,' said the manager helpfully, 'are those the ones you mean?' but the suggestion was met with a malevolent stare by the singer.

By the time they had finished the meal the club was packed. Lucerelli looked round approvingly. 'While she's on stage, man, we can suss out the talent.' The talent was mainly black which meant that Shula was assured of a good reception. Lucerelli traded on this, mentioning his connections with the singer to every girl he chatted up. His second sentence was usually 'Do you wanna screw?'

Knox winced at the technique. Having been something of a ladies' man in his bachelor days, albeit more in the Cary Grant mould, it was not what he was used to. He was about to advise the American that this was not the way to go about things in England when Lucerelli turned to him and introduced three girls whom, he said, would be coming back to the hotel with them. 'See you later girls,' he said when introductory French kisses had been exchanged and he ushered Knox to the back of the stage.

'How do you do it?' asked Knox. 'Weren't they insulted being asked outright like that if they wanted to screw?'

'Jeez, no man. You gotta have the technique. First you tell them you are with the pop star, get them interested. Then you tell them what you want them for and while they think about it you mention that there will be champagne and celebrities back at the hotel if they fancy partying a little.'

'Who are these celebrities exactly?'

Lucerelli roared with laughter and helped himself to a swig of cheap wine from a bottle thoughtfully given to him by the manager after he had kindly finished off the three meals. 'I know where my celebrity is. It's in my fucking trousers.' He laughed in an unbalanced way and wiped the surplus drink from his mouth with the back of his hand.

Knox smiled dutifully then, 'How did you come to meet Richard?' he asked, deciding this might be a good time to find out more about the drug set-up and hoping that the American's state of intoxication might have loosened his tongue.

'Lyn from the record company.'

'He's a friend of hers?'

'No, I don't think so. I think they just ring him when they want some stuff.'

'He gets anything then?'

'I think so. I don't really know. I just asked them where I could get my hands on some coke and Lyn said she would fix it. And this guy just came along.'

'Where does he live?'

Lucerelli looked at him sharply. 'Why all the questions? I dunno where he lives. I ain't set eyes on the guy before.'

'Just curious,' said Knox cautiously. 'I like to have a regular source of supply.'

'Don't you have your own contacts?'

'Oh sure but, like I said, this looked like good stuff.'

'That's right,' said Lucerelli. 'Listen man, we can have a really good scene going in that hotel tonight. We have the dope, these three chicks and that asshole up there.' He gesticulated towards Shula Sun who was signing autographs in the spotlight and kissing uplifted black cheeks like a Pope on a state visit. 'That's if you fancy it.' Both men groaned in unison.

In practice the orgy didn't go quite according to plan, much to Knox's relief as he strongly suspected that two of Lucerelli's trollops were suffering from advanced syphilis and he was not keen to catch it.

Shula Sun brought along two followers of her own. One was a black youth with a white satin shirt slashed to the waist to display a silver medallion bouncing against his smooth ebony skin; the other was a white boy who was obviously gay and seemed happy to bathe in Shula's glory and perhaps find out where she bought her false eyelashes.

After two hours of hard drinking, sniffing and smoking, the eight of them crammed in one bedroom, Lucerelli had passed out and was being openly fondled in his nether regions by two of the diseased girls, themselves almost naked after a brief interlude of strip poker.

Knox, who was an excellent poker player, watched in detached amusement. He was fully clothed.

The third girl was lovingly embracing Shula Sun who seemed to be quite taken with her advances and was reciprocating in like fashion, allowing her two escorts the opportunity to help themselves to the money and the cocaine in her handbag. Knox watched them rubbing powder furiously into their gums like overwrought dentists at a tooth festival.

Nobody noticed as he silently crept out of the room and returned to his own bedroom whence he rang the hall porter to bring him some Ovaltine.

'Bit of a noise next door,' he complained to that worthy.

'Noise!' ejaculated the porter, who was pleased to have someone to talk to at four in the morning. 'You want to see in there. There's a dozen of them, women as well. I've been up five times with different drinks.'

'Disgusting,' said Knox, relieved he hadn't been recognised.

'It's those pop stars, you know. All a bit funny in the head if you ask me. Too much money. Turns their brains.'

'Quite.' He tipped the man and settled down to his four hours rest. It was a hard life on the road.

Before the others were up next morning, he phoned Sergeant Evans from one of the public call boxes in the foyer and gave him a description of Richard.

'Somebody from the Drugs Squad should pick him out when they see the Identikit,' he said. 'I tried to place the accent but it was difficult. Maybe a trace of West Country.'

'Have you arranged to see him again?'

'On Boxing Day in Birmingham. Apparently he works with some band who are playing up there that night.'

'That won't go down well at home,' muttered Evans, who was a firm believer in family Christmases.

'Well this tour ends on the twenty-third, they go back to the States then, so at least I'll have Christmas Day at home.'

'And what is your plan with this Richard, sir?'

'Basically to persuade him I'm potentially a big buyer and need to see someone above him to negotiate favourable terms.'

'He's not suspicious of you at all?'

'He was at first and I think he could get nasty if he was crossed but he's only small fry. Too near the surface of things.'

'I'll get this picture done, anyway,' said Evans. 'Give me a ring in a day or two and I'll let you know what we come up with.'

Knox went into breakfast. He had finished his meal and read half the Daily Telegraph by the time the others appeared looking somewhat bedraggled.

'No time to dally,' he told them. 'We have to be in Cardiff in four hours.'

Lucerelli groaned. 'I just wanna go back to bed.' Shula had discarded her wigs to reveal a spiky crew cut which made her head look like a pumice stone with soot rubbed on it. Of the hangers-on only the white boy remained, pale as death and twitching in time to his pulse beat.

'What a sight,' sighed Lucerelli. 'I don't remember any of it so it must have been good. How many of those women did I have?'

'Two, and I had three,' lied Knox who did not want to appear ungrateful. 'I say, that coke of yours was really good.'

'Oh, we had that too did we?' He scratched fiercely under his hat then, with his thumb nail, carefully flicked the accumulated scurf from under his finger nails onto the hotel carpet. 'Jeez, some party eh? I told you it would be a good scene. I hope yo
u took some photos.' A fat old waitress approached with a menu. 'Hey, how long do we have to eat?'

'Two minutes. Cardiff is a long way.'

'What part of England is that in? Just give me some black coffee.'

'It's in Wales.'

'Oh, I see, a foreign country. Do they like the English or do they fight you like the Scots?'

Lucerelli's knowledge of British history was sketchy.

'They hate us. They burn our holiday homes and talk in a strange tongue if an Englishman is within fifty yards.'

The American looked alarmed. 'You better tell them I'm from the States, man. I don't wanna get killed in your country's tribal wars.'

'I think you might survive.'

Cardiff passed satisfactorily as did Bristol, Tyneside, Teesside and Glasgow. All the vouchers were distributed, Shula signed several hundred photos for people who had no idea who she was and Lucerelli consumed vast quantities of food. Local radio stations started to play the record.

Knox saw them off at Heathrow on the twenty-third.

'Thanks for everything, man,' said Lucerelli at the gate. 'I'll see you sometime, maybe next time without that asshole,' he whispered as Shula Sun returned from the magazine stand, arms laden with papers. She wore her red wig. She merely nodded as she passed, though Knox fancied he might have caught a muted 'Goodbye' as she flounced through the barrier.

He was glad it was all over. At last, he could have a quiet couple of days at home with Sue and her father.

However, it did not turn out to be a very quiet Christmas for Detective Chief Inspector Glass.

Chapter 7

Elliot Guthrie, alias 'The Hunter', sat in his office on December 23rd, trying to write his copy for the Christmas Eve edition of The Megaphone.

The big race of the holiday weekend was the King George VI Chase at Kempton Park. He fancied Lady Veronica again after her success at Newbury but a big threat came from the stablemate of Sailor's Delight, Little Sweetheart.

Since his success in selecting the winner of the Hennessy Cognac Gold Cup, Guthrie had returned to his former tradition of regular losers. Some punters were saying he was the most reliable tipster in Fleet Street. You could always rely on his tips to finish well out of the first three.

Once again the threat of dismissal loomed large.

He wondered how good Little Sweetheart was. Perhaps he should take a look at Bertie Beaton's stables. He knew them well for he had ridden for him occasionally in the latter days of his career in the saddle. He observed that John Haile was riding which meant Willie Leigh was still not fit although rumours were beginning to circulate about how 'ill' he was.

He checked with his colleagues. Course correspondent was going for The Punter. Jurex had napped Little Sweetheart. He would show them.

The Hunter went back to his desk and placed a clean sheet of paper in his typewriter. He would scoop them all. He typed his headline: *LADY VERONICA TO SCOOP CHRISTMAS POOL.*

Dermot Draper's Newbury betting shop was full on Christmas Eve as the punters placed their bets to add extra excitement to their holiday.

Finances were sliding since his £4,000 'win' on the Hennessy Cognac Gold Cup. He had had to provide a new car for his wife whose legs were not up to pedalling her Raleigh Traveller bicycle. His tax assessment was due in a week, as were his rates, shop rental and gas and electricity bills. There was also the matter of a private medical bill for the removal under anaesthetic of a deep-seated corn from his wife's little toe.

He could do with another small windfall.

He checked the books. There was a lot of money, £3,000 in fact, on Little Sweetheart to win the King George VI Chase, Little Sweetheart, like Sailor's Delight, being a local horse.

It was tempting. Should he keep the money, not lay a penny off, and chance it would lose?

He hesitated. If the horse went to the post at 4-1 he would end up owing over £15,000 if it won.

But if it never reached the finishing post…. He stroked his moustache.

It had worked once with Sailor's Delight.

Why not again?

Lord Crossens, having deserted the ancestral home north of the Border, lived with his current wife in a Tudor mansion in Gloucestershire. The original owners, forced out by escalating maintenance costs, had been relegated to a three bedroomed Wimpey house on an estate in Tewkesbury, a building smaller than their erstwhile garage.

The Earl had been married several times, showing a preference for very young brides qualified to be called 'society ladies' thanks to years of selective in-breeding.

The present incumbent of the position was one of the younger daughters of the Berkshire Norton-Smythes, who rejoiced in the name of Melinda Selina.

Melinda was an empty-headed girl with a braying laugh and prominent nostrils. She was an ex-point-to-point champion and both she and her husband were members of the local hunt, who considered themselves privileged to boast a title in their ranks and consequently said less than they might have done about His Lordship's 'vigorous' treatment of his horses.

The couple had no children of their own although Lord Crossens himself had accumulated five known offspring from various past alliances, none of whom he saw from one year to the next.

The couple spent Christmas Day alone, waited on by a small household staff comprising cook, butler and handyman/chauffeur.

On Boxing Day they planned to go to the race meeting at Kempton Park where Lord Crossens's horse, Little Sweetheart, was running in the King George VI Chase.

He fancied the horse had an excellent chance of winning, especially as his trainer had obeyed his instructions to replace Willie Leigh, the bungling jockey whose ineptitude had cost him the Hennessy Cognac Gold Cup.

He did not realise that, as Willie Leigh was still injured, the question had not really arisen.

He had left the choice of replacement to Albert Beaton. He did not know John Haile well but knew he had won a few good races. He'd better win this one, thought Lord Crossens, or there will be trouble. Nothing had to go wrong this time or he would want to know why. Heads would roll.

He sipped his Christmas port and looked forward to Boxing Day.

John Haile spent Christmas Day at the family farm in County Cork. He had three brothers and two sisters and, on Christmas morning, they all went riding on the downs.

John was described by the sporting papers as a 'promising young jockey'. They had referred to him as 'promising' ever since he graduated from point-to-points to win the Irish Grand National at Fairyhouse when he was nineteen, five years ago.

He had won the race again since then and his reputation had earned him several good rides on the other side of the Irish Sea, but he still remained 'promising'.

The main reason why he failed to fulfil that promise and win more major races was that John Haile was essentially unambitious. He was as happy riding in the fields with his family or with the local hunt as he was on a racecourse. As for money, as long as he had some in his pocket to spend, he was content.

In fact, he was even regretting that he had accepted Albert Beaton's offer to ride Little Sweetheart in the King George VI Chase the following day. Although the idea of winning one of the major races in the steeplechasing calendar appealed to him, so did Christmas at home with his family.

The person who telephoned must have had a fair conception of John Haile's character.

It was an Irish voice, one he did not recognise, and sounded more of a rasping whisper. 'If you win on Little Sweetheart tomorrow it will be your last ride. And if you call the police or tell anyone about this call, little Kirsty will suffer. And make sure you ride, mister. Just don't win.'

The line went dead. John Haile stared at the instrument in horror. Kirsty was his baby sister. She was only five years old and had a diseased hip which prevented her from walking properly. John spent hours taking her round the fields on her own Shetland pony.

He said nothing to the family about the call. He did not want to worry them. Neither did he go to the police station. He could not jeopardize his sister's safety. He dared not tell anyone in racing in case they informed the authorities.

The caller had his psychology right.

To a simple family boy like John Haile, there was only one practical solution. Winning a race was not as important to him as his family. He did not consider how the result would affect the owner, trainer or the punters. Even his anger at the unknown antagonist did not move him enough to try to trace him or take steps to have him brought to justice.

No, he would ride Little Sweetheart at Kempton Park.

And lose.

The Hunter did not think that Little Sweetheart would win the King George VI Stakes. In the Christmas Eve edition of The Megaphone he wrote:

LADY VERONICA TO SCOOP CHRISTMAS POOL

My choice for the King George VI Chase must be Lady Veronica who was my winning prediction earlier this month in the Hennessy Cognac Gold Cup. She has proved, in that race, that she has the measure of Reverend Shaker and I do not believe that Little Sweetheart, stable mate of Sailor's Delight, has the stamina to last the distance.

'Wrong again,' said Detective Chief Inspector Glass who, replete with Christmas turkey, was sitting by the fire reading the paper. On his feet were new pink slippers given to him for Christmas by his widowed friend, Mrs. Lewthwaite. He had removed the fluffy pom-poms.

'Pardon?' said Detective Chief Inspector Knox who was still at the table, a glass of port in his hand.

'The Hunter. He's tipped Lady Veronica again to win at Kempton tomorrow.'

'It must be his favourite horse,' said Sue. 'Didn't he give that at that race where Nikki Beaton's boyfriend fell?'

'Little Sweetheart will walk it and that is one of Bertie Beaton's horses too.'

'Why isn't Sailor's Delight running?'

'They're probably saving it for the National Trial at Haydock Park next month.'

He lit an after dinner cigarette. 'I don't suppose either of you two fancy a day at Kempton Park tomorrow?'

'I have to go to Birmingham,' Knox reminded him. 'On this drugs job.'

'Mmmmm. Is Jim Evans on duty?'

'Not today but he will be tomorrow.'

'You don't think anything is going to happen, do you?' asked Sue, remembering Nicola Beaton's visit.

'No, of course not,' said Glass innocently. He still had a feeling about that. 'Ah well, I suppose I can always watch it on television.'

'You are very interested in racing these days,' said Knox. 'I thought football was your game.'

'It is, but it won't be the same if the Rangers fall into the Second Division. I couldn't summon up the enthusiasm to watch teams like Oldham or Bournemouth after getting used to Everton and Tottenham. They don't have the same attraction, you know.'

'Can't see you joining the missing millions.'

'You don't know. I might take a fancy to this American Football. All these big buggers with shin pads up to their shoulders.'

Robin Knox left for Birmingham after lunch the next day, driving in an unmarked police car.

'I hope he'll be all right,' Sue said to her father as she made a pot of tea.

'Don't worry,' said Glass. He switched on the television for the afternoon's racing. 'He can take care of himself.'

He was in time to watch the preliminaries of the King George VI Chase. The commentator was interviewing Lord Crossens about the chances of his horse, Little Sweetheart. Lord Crossens thought it had a very good chance and said so.

'A lot of people are disappointed that your other famous horse, Sailor's Delight, is not running this afternoon. After all, Cheltenham Gold Cup winners have often done well in this race.'

'I have a more important target for him,' said the Earl bumptiously.

'Ah yes, the Grand National. Now, do you still regard it as being as important as it once was, in view of the fact that many of the top steeplechasers never appear in it, like Arkle for example?'

'To my mind, the National will always be the big one because of the tradition and because the prize money is the biggest.'

'And you are not frightened of risking your horses at those notorious fences? Remember, Alverton was killed there in 1979 and even Golden Miller only finished the course twice in seven attempts.'

'But Lanzarote died at Cheltenham so where is your argument?'

The commentator coughed and changed the subject. 'Have you any plans to run Little Sweetheart in the National?'

'No. The distance is too much for her. But she is entered for the Cheltenham Gold Cup.'

'How do you rate her chances?'

'She won't win,' said Lord Crossens with startling candour. 'Sailor's Delight will win it for the second year running.'

'But surely Sailor's Delight is running at Aintree instead?'

'Not instead, as well as. Only one horse has completed the double in the same year; that was Golden Miller in 1934. Sailor's Delight will be the second. Sailor's Delight is a better horse than Golden Miller.'

'You're certainly very confident, my Lord.' The remark was ignored.

'Furthermore, I would like to point out that, whatever you may say about the quality of the opposition at Aintree, the course is still the same and it's the course that the horse has to beat. Don't forget that.'

'Er, no.' The commentator lost his place on the script. 'Er, you have two separate training programmes for the two horses?'

'Of course. Sailor's Delight I am running at the Northern courses, the National trials at Carlisle and Haydock Park because Aintree is my main objective with him. Little Sweetheart may run in the Leopardstown Chase after this.'

'And you fancy her chances this afternoon?'

'Certainly.'

'He's a cocky bugger,' thought Glass as he poured himself a second cup of tea. 'But he's right.'

But then, neither of them knew about John Haile's telephone call.

Albert Beaton handed the reins of Little Sweetheart over to his jockey. 'Just keep her going nicely near the front,' were his instructions, 'then give her her head about four furlongs from home.'

John Haile nodded. He wished he were back home in County Cork. So much could go wrong. The horse might run away with him and win. If he fell 'accidentally', he might be killed. If he lagged behind too obviously there could be a Stewards' Enquiry and, in these days of video films, a horse could no longer 'get lost' out in the country.

His best bet was to keep up with the front-runners as instructed but somehow get left behind in the last stages when they all made their last dash for the winning post. Happily, the opposition was strong. Lady Veronica had recently won the Hennessy Cognac Gold Cup and The Punter had won last season's Whitbread Gold Cup. Reverend Shaker was also running and the bookmakers' prices reflected the fact that it could be a close finish between at least six well-fancied runners.

They rode out to the start. Little Sweetheart, as was her wont, took up the early running with two other horses. The seven-year-old mare usually ran at two and a quarter miles and this race was three miles but the course was flat and fast and often won by horses used to shorter distances.

At the end of the second mile Little Sweetheart was still up with the leaders. She jumped the fences, the stiffest outside Aintree, perfectly. Alongside her was Reverend Shaker, who had beaten her into second place in the Massey Ferguson Gold Cup at Cheltenham a fortnight ago, and the favourite, Lady Veronica.

Four furlongs from home and the race was open. John Haile took a deep breath as his mount thundered round the right-handed course. This was the moment he was expected to make his challenge. The thought of his sister, Kirsty, flashed into his mind. Instead of looking for a gap to push his horse through, he positioned himself behind the two horses, still racing hard but without a chance of breaking through to the front.

Lady Veronica won the race, a short head in front of The Punter who finished strongly and would have won had the distance been one furlong longer. Third was Reverend Shaker. Little Sweetheart was fifth, three lengths behind the winner.

Lord Crossens was furious. 'First that bungler Leigh falls off the best horse in Britain. Now this Irish cretin dallies about in the middle of the field like a novice at a gymkhana. In future, I'm going to ride my own bleddy horses.'

Albert Beaton, who bore the brunt of the Earl's wrath, was deeply chastened. John Haile had ridden for him before and always competently. Bertie felt the jockey should have been more alert or forceful in finding a way through the field but not every jockey was John Francombe or Jonjo O'Neill. Or, come to that, Willie Leigh but even he, it appeared, made the odd mistake. Certainly, Lord Crossens was unlikely to do any better.

John Haile felt sick. After the race he apologised to Bertie, murmuring something about 'being blocked in', and left the course for home. He did not feel able to indulge in social intercourse with the other jockeys and he wanted to make sure no harm had come to Kirsty. Luckily, nobody seemed to have suspected anything was wrong.

Even Glass, in front of his television set, viewed the defeat of his selection with equanimity. The Hunter had been right again. Another victory for Lady Veronica. Perhaps, thought Glass, he had better stick to doing the pools. Or start backing The

62

Hunter's selections. He lit another Craven A and waited for the next race.

But one person was not happy with the result of the King George VI Chase. Nicola Beaton's intuition was working overtime. She felt that there was something wrong with the race and she was determined to find out what it was.

So she rang Detective Chief Inspector Glass.

'You told me to ring you if anything suspicious happened.' Nicola was phoning from a call box at Kempton Park. Glass had been about to see the finish of the next race on television. But he was instantly alerted by Nicola Beaton's voice.

'What was it?'

'We had a horse running in the last race, I'm at Kempton Park'

'I know. I've been watching on television. Little Sweetheart. I thought it was going to win, I backed it.'

'That's the whole point. It should have won.'

'Now hang on a minute, Nikki, if all the horses that should win did win, bookmakers would be out of business.'

'There was something wrong, I know it. All right, it might have come second or third but that horse would not have been beaten by a rank outsider like that old nag that came fourth.'

Glass consulted his paper with the list of runners. ''Hot California Nights' you mean?'

Fallen three times out of five, couldn't race a milkman's cart. I tell you, Mr Glass, something is wrong.'

'Was the horse dope tested?'

'Yes. And the horse is fine. Never looked better, hardly panting.'

'The only alternative, then, is the jockey. Was he OK after the race? He didn't complain of blackouts or dizziness?'

'I hope you are not being sarcastic. No, he apologised to my father and mumbled something about not being able to find a gap through the other horses.'

'He did appear to be blocked in on television.'

'If he had taken up the running when he was told, he could have easily got through.' Nicola Beaton was not the sort of girl to suffer excuses.

'Is he normally a good jockey?'

'Average. Not up to Willie's standards but he's won a few good races. But he didn't do what Daddy asked him to do. Now, why?'

'Why do you think?' Glass was interested to know what the girl's sixth sense was telling her. The facts amounted to little but he was always prepared to listen to hunches.

Nicola was silent for a moment. It had all happened so fast, the race had not been over more than half an hour. She tried to crystallise into words the various reactions and observations circulating in her mind.

'I think,' she said slowly, 'that John Haile threw that race.'

'Why?'

'I don't know. But you're the detective. Will you help me find out?'

Glass sighed and stubbed out his cigarette on his saucer. 'I'm the busiest man in Scotland Yard, Nikki. I have a day off every two years. If I had more, the murder rate in the City would double within a week, there would be riots in Knightsbridge and not a bank in London would be safe.'

'What I'm asking you to do,' she said, ignoring his soliloquy, 'is this. Go and see this jockey, John Haile. Just one visit, that's all. If you get nothing from that then forget it. I shan't ring you again.'

'And if you're right and he did throw the race?'

'Then, Chief Inspector, you've got yourself a case.'

'Where does John Haile live?'

She hesitated. 'Ireland, I'm afraid.'

'Oh Christ. Out of the question. Look, I don't even have time to go to Loftus Road to see a football match, never mind Ireland. Anyway, I'm sick on planes.'

'But he'll be over here next week for the Cheltenham meeting. You could see him then. He's riding another of our horses.'

Glass demurred. 'That's more like it. I suppose I could manage half a day.'

'If your son-in-law can do it, I'm sure you can.' She mentioned she had met Detective Chief Inspector Knox at Nottingham.

Glass gave in. 'All right. I'll see you at Cheltenham, on the course. I don't know, I shall probably lose my pension over this. But don't let that worry you.'

'I won't. And ... thanks.'

Glass put down the phone. 'Is there any more tea in that pot?' he shouted to his daughter. Sue Knox brought it in and poured him a cup.

'Don't get up,' she said. 'Not on your old legs.'

'That was Nicola Beaton on the phone.'

'What did I tell you? I knew there was a reason for you wanting to go racing.'

'Not at all but it looks like she might be on to something and this time there is an easy way to find out.' He told her about John Haile.

'He did throw the race,' said Sue, after she had heard the story. 'There is nothing more certain. When you start getting hunches, something always happens.' She poured herself a cup of tea and sat in the armchair opposite. 'I wonder how Robin is getting on? I have a feeling too. I don't like this drugs thing he is on at all.'

But Detective Chief Inspector Knox was having a very boring afternoon.

Chapter 8

The M1 was almost clear of traffic on Boxing Day afternoon as Robin Knox drove up to Birmingham in the police Rover.

He was dressed in his record promoter's outfit of sweatshirt and jeans with his coney fur jacket. In the zipped up back pocket of his jeans he carried two hundred pounds in ten pound notes. The inside of the car was littered with record posters, publicity stickers and vouchers. He was back to being Jeremy Rowlands.

It was not difficult finding the Albany Hotel which was right on the ring road which circumnavigated the city centre.

He took his room key from the receptionist who informed him, in answer to his question, that nobody had been asking for him. He went up to his room to wait. It was five o'clock.

By seven o'clock there was no sign of Richard. He rang the switchboard to confirm that there was a show on at the Odeon Theatre that night.

'Yes, there's a concert on,' said the operator. 'Rotorhead, the heavy metal band from Australia.'

'Thanks.' He put the phone down and thought. The concert would commence at eight at the latest. He would give Richard another hour. He went down to the carvery for a meal, on the way asking the receptionist to page him if he had a visitor. Nobody came.

At eight fifteen, a large T-bone steak inside him, he walked across the city to the Odeon.

'I'm looking for someone with the band,' he told the doorman who directed him backstage. Here he found a couple of Rotorhead's roadies outside their truck, a blue and silver vehicle with their name emblazoned along the side.

'I'm looking for a guy named Richard,' he said. 'Supposed to be doing the lights for you.'

The two exchanged blank glances. 'Nobody of that name with us, Blue.'

'You are with Rotorhead?'

'Sure.'

'Is there another band on with you?'

'Yeah, some crappy punk outfit called The Demented Librarians.'

'Perhaps he's with them.'

'You're joking. They haven't even got synths never mind lights and the only guy with them is a bloke of fifty with white hair and shades, looks like Andy Warhol.'

'Doesn't sound like Richard but he did say he would be here tonight. He said he was the lighting engineer.'

'Sorry. Our lights man is from Australia like the rest of us.'

'Perhaps he is working for the theatre?'

'You could try but I shouldn't think so. They have their own regular staff, not one nighters.'

Knox thanked them and made enquiries at the front of the house. These confirmed that all the theatre staff were full time employees and none were called Richard.

'I reckon you've been sold a bum steer there, pal,' said the assistant manager to whom the detective's questions had been directed. 'I can't remember any Richards here and I have been here myself since 1979.'

Knox offered a description of the missing drug pusher but the response was the same. 'Not here.

Could you perhaps be confusing this place with the Town Hall? They have concerts on from time to time.'

'Tonight?'

'No, they are closed tonight.'

That was it then. He walked back to the hotel. 'No,' said the receptionist, still nobody had asked for him. She looked at him pityingly, imagining he had been stood up on a computer date. Knox settled his bill and walked to the car park adjoining the hotel. The receptionist watched him go. So much for his night on the town. She wondered if he was married but decided not. She would not have minded spending the night with him herself. He was good-looking and seemed to be connected with show business judging by his sweater. Fancy standing a bloke like that up. Now some of the old businessmen coming to the hotel on their 'liaisons' she could understand. Funny he had asked for a single room though. Perhaps he was shy.

Knox drove away from the city annoyed and frustrated. His only lead had gone. Had Richard deliberately lied? If so, was it because he specifically mistrusted him? Or had something happened to Richard to keep him from the appointment? Or any other appointment? An actuary would not give good odds for the survival rate of a drug pusher.

Cruising down the M1 at 70 mph, the detective considered his next move. He could try the record company. The girls there had first introduced Richard to Lucerelli. Failing that, he was back to square one. He pulled into the Watford Gap services to ring Sue and have a cup of tea.

'We'll wait up for you,' she said. 'We have more news than you have.'

Robin Knox arrived home at midnight. Detective Chief Inspector Glass told him of Nicola Beaton's phone call.

'You have still nothing to go on,' Knox said. 'Did I tell you I saw her at Nottingham?'

'No, but she did,' interposed Sue.

'Sorry, I forgot.'

'She said you looked scruffy but you were in disguise. You're not going in for false moustaches and waxed lips are you?' Her husband maintained a dignified silence.

'It seems to me that my case is progressing more than yours after all,' gloated Glass. 'So, what is your next move?'

'There is only the record company left. If nothing happens with that then I suppose I'll be back on normal duties.'

Knox went round to Trolfid Records three days later when they returned to work after the Christmas break.

'Is Lyn from Publicity in?' he asked the girl on the desk.

'She doesn't work here anymore.' The girl didn't look up and she spoke in the frosty manner of most London secretaries. 'She left to have a baby.'

'Who is there I can speak to from that department?'

'What do you want?'

Lyn's was the only name he knew. 'Let me go up and see them.'

'Sorry. Someone will come down if you tell me what you want.'

It took five minutes of quiet insistence before the policeman finally gained entrance to the Publicity Office. He recognised one girl who had been at Whites. She had red hair done in long ringlets like an American country singer or a Blackpool landlady.

'Remember me, Jes Rowlands? I was on the Shula Sun tour. We were at Whites Hotel together.'

'Oh yes. You were with the American guy, Frankie.'

'That's right. Listen, one of your crowd organised some dope for Frankie, some grass and some coke. A guy called Richard brought it up to Nottingham. Do you know where I can find him?'

'Sorry, no idea. He comes into the office from time to time and we get stuff from him but I don't know where he lives or anything. Hey you lot,' she shouted to the other girls in the office. 'Does anybody know how to get hold of Richard?'

'Richard who?' in chorus.

'You know, the guy with the coke.'

'Oh, that Richard.' Nobody knew how to reach him.

'Then how,' asked Knox, 'were you able to get some coke up to Frankie at Nottingham?'

'Easy. Richard had been in the office that day. We bought some grass off him and he said he would bring some coke in for us the next day. So we told Frankie we'd get some for him too. Richard delivered it himself.'

'Richard was supposed to get some for me last week,' said 'Jeremy Rowlands', but he didn't show up.'

Nobody seemed surprised. 'If we see him we'll tell him you were looking for him,' said the redhead. 'Has he got your number?'

'I'm on tour for a month,' lied the detective. 'Tell him to leave a message at Whites. And to let me know where I can contact him.' He walked to the door and stopped. 'Didn't Lyn have his number?'

'I don't think so. She just knew him like the rest of us, through coming in here.'

'OK. See you.'

Knox reported back to the Yard where he had a meeting with the Assistant Commissioner and Superintendent Page from the Drugs Squad.

'Anything odd about this girl Lyn leaving the record company?' asked Page.

'No sir. Apparently she was pregnant.'

'So they just take pot luck, as it were.' The officer smirked to himself at his little quip, 'And buy the stuff whenever they can.'

'That's about it, sir.'

'This fellow seems to turn up on the doorstep just like a brush salesman,' said the Assistant Commissioner.

'More successful I think,' said Page, icily. 'You don't get hooked on brushes.'

'You don't get hooked on cannabis either,' said Knox who was in favour of banning tobacco instead.

'But you do get hooked on cocaine and the idea of these young office girls being able to obtain it so easily, well frankly it terrifies me.'

'Tell me,' said the Assistant Commissioner, 'do you think this American chap knew how to find this Richard?'

Knox shook his head. 'I shouldn't think so. He reckoned the girls introduced him and the only time they met was in Nottingham.'

'To your knowledge.'

'Yes, but I was with Lucerelli practically all the time. Besides, he is back in America anyway.'

'That's true. Well, until we can find another way in, you might as well revert to normal duties for the time being, Chief Inspector. Your sergeant will be glad; he has been complaining of overwork.'

'What happened?' enquired Detective Chief Inspector Glass when his son-in-law returned home.

'Back to work as per usual. Apparently Sergeant Evans is collapsing under the strain.'

'Case over, eh?' Glass sniggered. He handed across a copy of The Megaphone folded open at the racing page. 'Take a look at that; Saturday's paper.' Knox read.

ANOTHER VICTORY FOR THE HUNTER

Our star tipster The Hunter landed another nap yesterday when Lady Veronica won the King George VI Chase at Kempton Park. This is the second time that The Hunter, alone amongst racing forecasters, has correctly selected the Irish horse to win a big race in the space of one month. Yes, The Megaphone has the men that matter and today . . .

'So what?' said Knox.

'Just thought it was odd that's all. Twice he has picked a horse that has had no chance and twice it's won.'

'Which is what he is paid to do.'

'But the other hundred odd races he hasn't done it. Is it just a coincidence that the two races where horses have been nobbled . . . ?'

'We don't know they have and it was the jockeys not the horses.'

'The two cases are the two times he wins.'

'Clutching at straws I'd call it. You can't really suspect him? You'll be saying it was Ladbrokes next.'

'I'm considering bookmakers,' replied Glass. He lit a Craven A. 'You will be sorry to hear that I'm returning home on Friday.'

'Your landlady missing you?'

'Huh. That old slattern. She has probably sub-let my rooms to holidaymakers.' He looked around the spacious lounge, furnished in a Scandinavian style yet still retaining the art deco atmosphere of Robin Knox's bachelor flat in Portman Square. 'Not a bad place this. I could retire here.' He sighed theatrically. 'And it won't be many years away the way my old bones ache.'

'It will be next week if you don't solve more cases. When is it you are going to see this jockey?'

'Wednesday. At the Cheltenham meeting. That will be the day, Robin, when I know whether or not I have got a case.' He smiled to himself. 'And my bet is I will have.'

Chapter 9

Detective Chief Inspector Glass took his sergeant, Moon, with him to Cheltenham. 'The fresh air will do you good lad, you've been looking a bit peaky lately.'

They drove in Glass's 'new' car, a Mini Countryman, his previous collector's item having had a long delayed permanent seizure in a lay-by off the A5 at Edgware.

'This is not official,' he warned. 'Just a bit of a nose round.'

'The local police will not be happy.'

'Neither will the Jockey Club but as they're not involved at this stage either, there is no need to tell them.'

Moon yielded to his superior's irrefutable logic.

'Besides,' added Glass, 'I took the trouble to book us both an afternoon off duty, just to cover us.'

'Oh good,' said Moon, glumly. He had intended to use his next day off to visit his fiancée's sick mother in the Armageddon Nursing Home.

'Don't mention it. I hope you like racing.'

'Mmm.' The sergeant was tactful enough not to risk ruining the day out but he was not impressed with the 'case' as presented to him. 'Not much to go on, is there?' was his only comment and privately he thought it was an excuse for his superior to go to the races.

Here he misjudged his man. Glass had a nose for potential cases and never more than in this instance.

Taking the M4 up to Swindon, they arrived in time for the first race. Despite the arctic December wind, the course was reasonably full and it took them some little time to locate the Beatons unloading their horse from its box. Glass introduced his sergeant and Nicola greeted them warmly but Albert looked uncertain.

'Nikki has only just told me why she has asked you down here, Walter. I can't say I'm happy about it. If Haile was to complain . . . .'

'Don't worry, Bertie. I'm noted for my diplomacy,' lied Glass. 'If he is innocent, he'll have nothing to complain about.'

'And if he's guilty? If he did lose that race?'

'Then I'll find out. He'll not hide anything from me.' Moon nodded his agreement. At the Yard, they said that Glass had trained with the Spanish Inquisition.

'Well, you know best Walter. I'll leave it to you.'

The inspector nodded at the horse. 'Which one is that?'

'Cresswell Manor. John Haile is riding him.'

'Is he the favourite?'

'Oh no. It's a pretty open race. We've a fair chance though.'

'Who owns him?'

'He belongs to a syndicate. Businessmen looking for a tax loss. They claim the expenses against advertising. Cresswell Manor is a brand of mustard.'

'Does Lord Crossens have any horses other than those you train?'

'No. We have them all.'

'I see. Just looking for common factors. Who owns Lady Veronica?'

'Tom Ball, the financier. Eamonn Houghton is his trainer.'

'Unlikely to be anything there then. It's just that Lady Veronica won on both occasions.'

'Probably coincidence. The Punter would have had the King George in another ten yards.'

'Who owns The Punter?'

'Mrs. Peggy Bolton, widow of the chemical magnate. Goes to Ascot in ridiculous hats and still wears mini skirts at eighty-six. Her horses do well though. Ernie Coar trains them. Nothing funny there, Walter.'

Glass remembered The Hunter. 'What do you know about that bloke from The Megaphone who tipped Lady Veronica to win?'

'Guthrie you mean? He rode for me years ago, just before he retired when I was first starting up.'

'Was he good?'

'A champion. Until the booze got hold of him.'

'It still has. He doesn't pick many winners these days.'

'Except Lady Veronica, is that what you were going to say?'

Glass shrugged. 'Could it be significant?'

'I can't see it. Even if he had nobbled my horses there was no guarantee Lady Veronica would have won.'

'How about bookies?'

'More likely. They would have taken a caning if Sailor's Delight had won. You are looking really for the small man, couple of shops and low reserves. Probably someone local. There would be a lot of money on him round Newbury.'

'I'll bear that in mind. Thanks Bertie.'

'You'll wait until after the race to see Haile?'

'Don't worry, I won't ruin your chances. He'll probably want to do well to make up for Boxing Day. Do you fancy a bet Sergeant?'

Moon shook his head. Ethel, his fiancée, didn't approve of gambling.

'You'll get 8-1 on the course,' said Bertie Beaton.

Glass handed round a red packet of Craven A but nobody took one. 'What is Haile like?' he asked, striking a Swan Vesta.

'Quiet,' replied Nikki. 'Polite. Not a pushy sort of person.'

'Would he frighten easily?'

She looked up sharply. 'Probably. What are you going to do to him?' Moon wondered the same thing and wished he was at the Armageddon Nursing Home.

'Not me. Someone else. Because if he threw that race he did it on instructions. So he was either frightened or paid. Is he well off?'

Bertie supplied the answer. 'He's not interested in money. I've known him turn down good rides because he wanted to stay at home with his folks, hunt with the local hounds, that sort of thing.'

'So someone got at him. Unless, of course, it was all his idea. Has he got any grudge against you or anyone else that you know of?'

'No. We've always been on good terms. He is a very affable fellow. See for yourself.'

'I will,' said Glass. 'And now we'll let you get on. I'll talk to Haile after the race then perhaps we could come up to your place this evening. Is that OK?' The Beatons nodded. 'Come along, Sergeant.

78

We'll go and make my fortune for the afternoon. I think I can risk a pound each way on Mr.Haile.'

Glass won £10 as Cresswell Manor, watched by BBC cameras, ran home a good length clear of the rest of the field.

'A good omen,' he said to Moon as he collected the pound notes from the course bookmaker and prepared to find John Haile.

The jockey was coming out of the owners' enclosure when the detective laid his bulky arm on his shoulder.

'Mr Haile?'

'Yes?'

'I am a police officer. Detective Chief Inspector Glass from Scotland Yard. I should like to ask you a few questions.'

'Me?' The voice was a tone higher.

'You are not racing in the next are you?'

'No, but. . .'

'Good. Let's go for a walk round the course then. The exercise will do my sergeant good.' He propelled the smaller man, still in his silks, to the perimeter of the course with Moon taking pace a step behind them.

'What's all this about?' They moved through several groups of people until, by the first fence, they were virtually alone.

'Right,' said Glass at last. 'Nobody about to hear us now. I'm giving you a chance, son.' He stopped walking and looked the jockey in the eye. 'I want to know why you deliberately lost the King George VI Chase at Kempton Park last Friday.'

Haile stuttered. 'I don't know what you're talking about.'

'No lying. I know you threw that race. Sergeant Moon there knows it. What we don't know and what you are going to tell us is why.'

'I was hemmed in, I tried to win.' But it was a tone of desperation, of a frightened man trying to talk his way out of trouble.

'Glass nudged him against the rail causing him to stumble. 'Let's have no messing about, Haile. I can have your licence for this. Now it was not money so my guess is someone threatened you so tell me all about it. Now.' He barked the last word and Haile jumped. Glass faced him, like a rattlesnake waiting to pounce. His eyes remained on Haile's face, his will stronger.

Haile started to cry. 'I didn't want to do it. He said he would kill my sister. She is crippled. She is only a baby.'

'All right son.' Glass put an arm round him, suddenly fatherly. 'Who was he?'

'I don't know.'

'What did he look like?'

'I never saw him. He phoned.'

'So. What did he sound like?'

'He had an Irish accent, a bit stronger than mine if you know what I mean.' Now that he had confessed, the jockey was eager to talk out of sheer relief.

'Easiest accent in the world to copy since Terry Wogan took over all the country's airwaves. "Hello dere Clancy! Will yo' be wantin' some tarmac off me lorry today?" yodelled Glass to a startled Sergeant Moon, in an unrealistic impression of a Belfast labourer.

'Yes, just like that,' agreed Haile, anxious to foster the detective's sudden excursion into joviality. 'Except he whispered.'

'A whispering Irishman eh? The worst kind.'

Haile pointed out that he himself was Irish but Glass waved aside his protests. 'I won't hold it against you lad,' he said, good humoured now his hunch had been proved correct. 'Now then, what did this man tell you to do? I suppose it was a man? A lot of women sound like men these days.'

'It sounded like a man. He just said I had to take part in the race but make sure I didn't win. And I had to tell nobody or he would get Kirsty.'

'Did he say why he wanted you to lose?'

'No.' He looked worried. 'What will happen now that I have told you? He might try to hurt Kirsty.'

'I shouldn't think he'll bother now. He's got what he wanted. Was it a coin box he called from, this whispering Paddy? No offence.'

'There were no pips.'

'Mmm. When did he ring?'

'Christmas Day.'

'Who knew you would be at home then?'

'I made no secret of it.'

'Mmmmm,' said Glass again. He could not think of anything else to say. His hunch had proved correct but the chances of tracing the phone call were nil. Haile obviously was telling the truth but all he was left with was a complete dead end. 'Shall we walk back?' he said. 'My legs aren't what they were and the wind is playing havoc with my rheumatism.'

'What will happen to me?'

'I don't know the Jockey Club rules but they will have to be informed. This could be part of a big conspiracy.' Glass did not know quite how. 'But I imagine they'll be lenient with you in view of what you've told me.'

They reached the main enclosure. 'You'll be hearing from me,' said Glass. 'And if you think of anything else that might help us or if the man gets in touch with you again, let me know at once. I'll be at the Yard.'

The two policemen walked back to the car park. 'I fancy a cup of tea after that,' said Glass. 'There's a little teashop I know in Broadway, not too far out of our way.'

'So you were right,' said Moon as they drove off along the A46 Stratford Road. 'What's the next move?'

'First of all I want to speak to Lord Crossens, he owns both horses. Then, maybe, we'll find a destitute bookmaker somewhere although I thought they only existed in cheap novelettes. Also, I fancy I might go to see Guthrie at The Megaphone. I could perhaps give him a bit of advice. Jim Evans picks more winners in a week than he does in a season.'

'Will we be long at the Beatons?' enquired Moon, changing tack.

'I should not think so, why? Had you got something planned?'

'Well, it is New Year's Eve, sir. I had promised to take Ethel out to a dinner dance at this hotel near us.'

'That's all right then. We should be home by eight.'

They partook of tea and scones at the Small Talk teashop in Broadway, then drove through Chipping Norton to the Beatons.

Bertie Beaton's house was a nineteenth century farmhouse adjoining the stables, both built in the traditional local stone which made the countryside round The Cotswolds look warm even in the depths of winter.

'I'm about to serve dinner,' Nicola Beaton greeted them. 'I hope you'll both join us.' Sergeant Moon was about to protest but Glass was in first. 'Delighted,' he smiled. 'Very kind.'

Willie Leigh was another guest at the meal and he was delighted to hear the policeman's news.

'I'd begun to wonder if I was imagining things,' he said.

'How could Haile let us down like that?' stormed Nicola.

Her father sipped his game soup philosophically.

'Understandable in the circumstances, I suppose.'

'Nonsense, he ought to have had more backbone.' Glass thought Nicola Beaton's backbone would have supported Tower Bridge.

Dinner was a four course affair with ample wines and spirits. By the time the sherry trifle was served, Sergeant Moon was becoming red-faced and slurring his words. Glass, who was used to strong drink, merely became verbose.

'You have not encountered further suspicious circumstances?' he enquired of Willie Leigh.

The jockey shook his head. 'But then, I've not been riding.'

'They might not have waited until you boarded a horse.'

'Mounted,' corrected Nicola. 'You board buses.'

'Are you going to arrest Haile?' asked Bertie.

'I am seeing the Jockey Club on Monday. I'm concerned with the person or persons behind it all.'

Moon became fidgety during the coffee but quietened down when port was served and, by the time they came to leave at nine o'clock, he was somnambulant.

'We will have to go,' said Glass at last. 'Sergeant Moon has an assignation with his affianced. I'll give you a ring in a week or so.' He paused at the door. 'I asked you if either of you had any enemies that you could think of, didn't I?'

Father and daughter looked at one another and together answered 'No'.

'No we haven't, that is,' explained Bertie. 'Not that we know of anyway.'

'If you have, be sure I'll find them,' said Glass. 'This case is just starting.'

They drove to London at the fastest speed the Mini Countryman could attain which was 65 mph.

'I hope you can manage a second meal,' said the Chief Inspector as he dropped Moon off at Ethel's home. 'Happy New Year.'

Glass himself didn't go back to his daughter's. Instead he went straight to the Compton Road Welfare and Social Club where he was in time for a finger buffet, the raffle and live music from the Jesse James Quartet.

He spent the night in a red-bricked semi in a tree-lined street near Wembley, home of his widowed friend Mrs. Lewthwaite.

Chapter 10

Elliot Guthrie alias The Hunter was busy in The Megaphone offices when Detective Chief Inspector Glass and Sergeant Moon arrived. He was cogitating over his selection for the Lucius Handicap Chase at Carlisle.

Once again, as in the Hennessy Cognac Gold Cup, every tipster in the country had napped Sailor's Delight. He searched hopefully through the remaining runners but there was not one horse amongst them that had a particularly outstanding chance of being second. They shared a common mediocrity and only the excessive weight imposed by the handicapper was likely to beat the 8-11 favourite.

'So this is where men's dreams of fortune are ruined,' sighed Glass. Guthrie looked up to see a large man in a shapeless greatcoat standing beside his desk. Behind him was a thin, younger man with a bland face and pudding basin haircut. 'You are The Hunter, forecaster of losing horses for The Megaphone?'

'Who the hell are you?'

An identity card was flashed before his eyes. 'Detective Chief Inspector Glass, Scotland Yard.' Glass studied the other's face. It was well lined, the eyes deeply etched and the nose prominent, like a Capo-di-Monte figurine. Broken veins under the skin indicated substantial alcohol consumption.

'What can I do for you? You looking for a tip?'

'Last place in the world I'd come if I was. When did you last pick a winner, was it Arkle in 1965?'

'Have you just come here to insult me, Chief Inspector?'

'No. I've come to ask you what your secret is.'

'What secret?'

'The secret of your two wins this year. How you alone, of all the Fleet Street oracles, should predict that Lady Veronica would win the Hennessy Cognac Gold Cup.'

'I'm paid to pick winners.'

'You're being paid too much then.' Glass observed with interest the purple patchwork of veins on the man's neck, rising and falling in anger. 'The thing is, Lady Veronica shouldn't have won that race.'

'That's rubbish. There is no such thing as should in racing.'

'Sailor's Delight should have won that race and would have if. . .?'

'If what?'

'On Boxing Day you picked Lady Veronica again, to win the King George.'

'And it did. Oh, don't tell me. It shouldn't have done.'

'Quite right. Little Sweetheart should have won.'

'But it didn't, did it?'

'Did you ever wonder why?'

'I know why. Lady Veronica reached the post first. Now have you finished with these ridiculous questions?'

'Somebody, Mr.Guthrie, fixed it so that Sailor's Delight and Little Sweetheart did not win. Somebody who had, what you might call, a vested interest.'

'Are you suggesting…?'

'I'm merely putting forward a hypothesis,' said Glass, 'that a racing correspondent, who would have a job to forecast the winner of the Boat Race after Oxford had sunk, might find it in his interest to, shall we say, arrange the outcome of a race.'

Guthrie jumped up from his seat and made to strike the detective. 'Now look here. . . .' he began but Glass merely brushed him aside.

'Calm down, Mr.Guthrie. Like I say, only a hypothesis.'

'Wait a minute. Let's get this straight. You're saying that somebody prevented those two horses from winning, right?' The policeman nodded. 'And I had a motive in that I had selected a different horse to win?'

'Lady Veronica.'

'Quite. Well, tell me, Chief Inspector,' his voice taking on a biting edge, 'did I also get at the other horses in those two races, because any of them could have beaten Lady Veronica?'

'Maybe, but those two horses were the main dangers.'

'Granted. But I was the only correspondent in Fleet Street who tipped Lady Veronica. The others gave a variety of horses and then only as place bets. Mine were naps.'

'Even so . . .' Glass was on the defensive.

'Even so . . . I could hardly have nobbled the whole field.'

Glass thought for a moment and conceded to himself that The Hunter maybe had a point but he didn't want to admit defeat. Instead, he asked the other man for his opinion on the case, always a good ploy, he felt, when the interrogation was getting out of hand.

'It strikes me,' volunteered Guthrie, that instead of looking for somebody who wanted that particular horse to win, you should be looking for someone who wanted Sailor's Delight and Little Sweetheart to lose. A bookie maybe.'

'I'd considered that,' said Glass haughtily. He took out his cigarettes and offered one to The Hunter who accepted. 'I don't suppose you've heard any whispers yourself, bookies on the skids?'

'I wouldn't do here, would I? I'm out of touch with the grass roots as it were. In fact I'm out of touch with most of it these days,' he added almost sorrowfully. 'Lady Veronica was a desperate gamble that came off.'

'We all have bad patches,' said Glass sympathetically. Moon noted with interest how all the Chief's interviews seemed to start belligerently and ended up with Glass consoling the erstwhile suspect. 'Times when nothing seems to go right.' Moon feared Glass was going to offer him money.

'It's the drink, you know.' Guthrie was becoming maudlin. 'Can't keep off the bottle.'

'It's a demon,' agreed Glass, whose own consumption of Southern Comfort would have done justice to a Mississippi paddleboat captain. 'Luckily it never affects me.'

'That's that,' he said to Moon as they left the newspaper office. 'What's next?'

'Lord Crossens,' replied Moon. 'What do we know about him?'

'Millionaire twice over, started off in jam then branched into the city. One of the top racehorse owners last season. Likes the women I believe.'

'Is he married?'

'Five times. Which means, if he started at about twenty, he gets through one every four years. Long enough for a wife that, what do you say, Sergeant?'

Moon ignored the question. 'I can't see him doing a swindle, then.'

'Enough money already, you mean? You may be right. Could be a grudge job though.'

'Do you think so?'

'No, not really. I think it will be a dead end like all the rest. He'll be a worried owner, unable to understand why his expensive racehorses keep on losing.'

There he was wrong. Lord Crossens was not so much worried as angry when the two policemen called to impart the news of Willie Leigh's doping. And his anger turned to wild fury when they told him of John Haile's misdemeanour.

'I'll have the beggar warned off. He'll never ride in England again. Let him get back to the other side of the swamp where he belongs.' He glared at Glass. 'I trust you're going to find out who is behind all this, Chief Inspector?'

'I was hoping you might be able to give me a few hints, sir.'

'How the hell would I know? It's your job to find out these things. That's what the country is paying you for.'

'I know it's unlikely,' persisted Glass, sweetly, 'but have you any enemies or people you have had a disagreement with lately?'

'Nobody at all. Any enemies I have don't have the guts to do anything but talk behind my back.'

'Do you back your own horses?'

'What has that got to do with it?'

'Simply that you might have backed them to lose in which case I might have a fair case for arresting you,' said the detective, eschewing tact in favour of shock tactics. The nobleman's face contorted like a punctured concertina.

'What the hell are you suggesting? By God, I'll have your stripes for this. Bleddy impertinence.'

'I take it the answer is no,' nodded Glass, equably. Injured pride and protested innocence bored him.

'I had two thousand pounds on Sailor's Delight and fifteen hundred on Little Sweetheart. You can check with William Hill. Both to win.'

'William Hill's are your regular bookmakers?'

'My only bookmakers.'

'So you had nothing to gain by your horses losing and you haven't an enemy in the world. Just coincidence, do you think, that you owned both these horses?'

'Probably another twenty horses have been got at that are nothing to do with me.' Glass thought that this might well be true. 'Obviously some crooked syndicate at work.'

'That, of course, is the most likely explanation,' agreed the Chief Inspector. 'But we have to explore all avenues of enquiry. The taxpayer expects it.'

They took their leave, driving the short distance to Cheltenham where they lunched at the Queen's Hotel.

'It will be an impossible task finding out if any other horses have been got at,' said Moon.

'Not impossible,' corrected his superior, 'but unlikely enough to discourage us from looking. There are other cases to solve. All we can do with this one is wait until something else turns up. We may get a whisper from someone.'

It was the detective's favourite course of action. Sit back at Scotland Yard and wait for Eddie the Nose to ring.

In this case, Eddie the Nose turned out, not unexpectedly, to be Nicola Beaton.

Chapter 11

'I've heard a few rumours,' said Nicola. 'So I thought I ought to ring you in case you want to investigate.'

'Quite right,' approved Glass, leaning back in his chair and putting his feet up on his paper-laden desk. 'I was on the point of giving up. Where are you?'

'Carlisle.'

'Carlisle?'

'Sailor's Delight is running today in the Lucius Handicap Chase.'

'Oh that's right, I'd forgotten. I meant to back him.'

'I shouldn't bother. The price isn't worth it. Listen, have you come across a bookie called Dermot Draper?'

'Can't say I know the name.'

'He has a shop in Newbury.'

'Just the one?'

'As far as I know. And apparently, it's not doing too well.'

'Isn't it, by Jove?'

'Hanging on from day to day, so they tell me. But he did do well out of the Hennessy when Sailor's Delight lost.'

'What about the King George?'

'I don't know about that but I thought it might be worthwhile you having a nose round.'

'You've done very well, Nikki.' His methods were vindicated again.

'Is Willie riding Sailor's Delight today?'

'No,' she answered shortly.

'Ah well, these things take time.'

'The owner is riding.'

'Lord Crossens? I don't believe it.'

'Why not? He is the owner. It's his privilege. After John Haile he says he doesn't trust jockeys any more.'

'Is he any good?'

'Oh yes, he can ride. He's won loads of amateur races but that's not quite the same thing. He's talking about riding in the Gold Cup.'

'That's not until March. Willie will be better by then, surely?'

'We'll have to see what happens.'

'What's the weather like up there?' asked Glass.

'Quite mild for January. The going should be good. There's been no rain for three or four days.'

'Best of luck then and thanks for the tip. I'll let you know how we get on at Newbury.'

'We seem to be spending a lot of time on this case,' murmured Sergeant Moon as they journeyed West once more on the M4.

'Don't we?' agreed the Chief Inspector, amicably. 'Let's hope we eventually solve it or there will be some explaining to do.'

They reached Newbury in under two hours and Glass made straight for the Chequers Hotel. 'I think we'll have lunch first,' he said. He was partial to expense account life and always bemoaned the fact that it was not he who had been asked to fly to South America to retrieve Ronnie Biggs from the sun-baked beaches of Brazil.

The hotel restaurant overlooked a secluded garden. Glass selected a table near the window and settled back in his chair to read the morning paper.

'I see The Hunter has stopped picking outsiders.' He handed the back page to the sergeant who read 'Sailor's Delight a cert at Carlisle.'

'He's right, of course. We must make sure we get to Draper's in time to back it.'

They ate abundantly, finishing off with tea and chocolate profiteroles.

'I must say that duck went down very nicely,' said Glass, struggling to fasten his greatcoat across his swollen belly. Sergeant Moon had to agree that the veal, too, had been quite tasty. Working with the Chief Inspector did have its advantages, not the least being Glass's inclination to go chasing round the country at the slightest excuse. Perhaps he had a part-time job with Egon Ronay that he had not disclosed at Scotland Yard. Certainly it was more congenial and less dangerous than wandering round the East End like other members of the Flying Squad seemed to do.

'We'll walk down,' said Glass. 'Get some off your weight.'

The little betting shop was situated in a side street between a greengrocer's, whose boxes of fruit and vegetables adorned the pavement, and a run down snack bar. A sign, 'D.R.Draper - Commission Agent', hung from chains in the middle of the blacked out window.

'Hardly Las Vegas,' commented Glass, opening the door and thereby activating a mechanical bell. Inside, rows of sporting papers lined the walls on either side with a shelf running along at navel height to accommodate pencils and betting slips for the punters to write out their selections.

Only the sporadic crackling announcements from a radio giving latest information from the courses differentiated it from the reading room of a public library, even down to the only two customers, unshaven old men in dirty raincoats without belts.

At the end of the shop, behind the grill, was a small man in a houndstooth suit, red bow tie and white shirt, attire that twenty years earlier would have marked him out as a dandy.

'Mr.Draper?'

'That is me, yes.'

'Detective Chief Inspector Glass, sir. Scotland Yard. Might I have a word with you in private please?' Although he spoke affably, Glass made the request sound like an invitation to face a firing squad.

Draper's face took on an expression of instant terror like that of a small boy who realises he has had an accident in his trousers. The detective was too experienced, though, to read anything into this. He knew that most perfectly innocent people, when confronted by the police, are seized by the irrational fear that they have unwittingly committed a heinous crime for which they are about to be arrested and sentenced to life imprisonment.

'What about?'

'In private if you don't mind.'

Draper summoned a young girl from behind the partition, unlocked the door at the side of the grill and ushered the detectives into the back of the shop.

'We are enquiring into the results of two races that have taken place in the last six weeks, both of them won by Lady Veronica.'

'Really.'

'The Hennessy Cognac Gold Cup and the King George VI Chase.'

Draper looked down at his crocodile skin shoes, a gesture not missed by the detective.

'I see these races mean something to you. Did you win much on them?'

'Er, I've no idea offhand, Chief Inspector. I would have to consult the books.'

'To the nearest thousand pounds will do. No need to go into detail.'

Draper licked his lips. He appeared to be having trouble salivating. 'Probably three or four,' he ventured, then caught Glass's steady glare. 'Maybe five.'

'Did you back Lady Veronica yourself?'

'No. The money came from bets placed on the losers.'

'Let me guess. Sailor's Delight for one.'

'It's a local horse, naturally there was a lot of interest in the town.'

'Naturally. Lucky for you that it lost really, although, of course, you had laid off some of the bets?'

'Not all of them.' Glass raised his Machiavellian eyebrows. 'The art of good bookmaking, Chief Inspector, is knowing when to lay off bets.' He gave a nervous little laugh.

'Only a cretin would have stood bets on Sailor's Delight, Mr.Draper. Or someone who knew in advance it was not going to win. Well-off are you?'

'What?' The bookmaker was startled by his interrogator's sudden tirade.

'Rumour in the town suggests you are in trouble. Had to sell your car, short of the readies, cash flow and liquidity problems I believe it is called nowadays.'

'Rubbish. I'm perfectly solvent.'

'But you might not have been if Sailor's Delight and Little Sweetheart had won those two races.'

'What is the nature of this enquiry?'

'Somebody fixed those races and made sure those horses didn't win. Was it you?'

'Good God, no. Look, I'll admit that I took a risk holding on to the bets but, well yes, I hadn't had such a good season so I took a chance on getting some of my money back.'

'A big chance wasn't it?'

'All right, yes, it was a big chance. But I was desperate.'

'Funny,' remarked Glass to his sergeant, 'how many desperate people we seem to encounter in this case.'

'The bills were mounting up, my creditors were pressing. It just so happened that a lot of extra money was placed on those particular races. The Hennessy Gold Cup is run here in Newbury and, like I said, it was a local horse. . . .'

'Yes, yes. I know all that.'

'But there is no way I could have influenced the result. How could I?'

Glass could think of several ways but, looking at the little man, none seemed likely.

'We may want to speak to you again,' was his parting comment.

They left the little shop and walked back to the hotel to pick up the Mini Countryman. 'Damn,' said Glass. 'I forgot to put a bet on Sailor's Delight. Never mind. What did you think of him?'

'Very unlikely that he would have the spirit to attempt the crime.'

'I agree. Waste of time. Everything in this case just comes to a dead end. All the avenues of enquiry have been exhausted. All we know is that a crime has been committed, in fact, several crimes. Fraud, attempted murder, on Willie Leigh. . . .'

'I doubt if you would make that stick, sir.'

'Silence. I was just cataloguing the offences. As we have nobody in mind to apprehend it hardly matters whether or not we would make them stick.'

'Perhaps it's part of a big racecourse fraud.'

'Oh, brilliant thinking, Moon. You'll make a traffic warden yet. Perhaps you would like to enlighten me as to how it works. No big money was put on either of the stricken animals to lose.'

'Mmmmmm.' Moon decided to keep quiet in future. The Chief Inspector switched on the car radio for the rest of the journey back and his mood was not lightened when it was announced on Radio Two's Sports Desk that Sailor's Delight had won the Lucius Handicap Chase at Carlisle. Without his money on it.'

'This case is finished for me,' he declared. 'Until there is another 'accident'.'

But plenty was to happen before that.

Chapter 12

Enquiries into the running of the Hennessy Cognac Gold Cup and the King George VI Chase were halted as Detective Chief Inspector Glass was kept busy with other cases.

The Jockey Club suspended John Haile subject to its own investigations and enquiry.

On February 6th Sailor's Delight with Lord Crossens up won the Haydock Park National Trial Handicap Chase which shortened still further its price for the Grand National.

Meanwhile, in America, Shula Sun's record, 'Reminisce About The One You Miss', attained the coveted Number One position on the Billboard Hot Hundred Chart.

Detective Chief Inspector Knox, back to normal duties, received no word from his cocaine supplier, Richard, who had been identified from his description as Richard Marchant. Instructions from the Drugs Squad were to leave well alone for the time being.

On February 16th, after extensive local radio airplay, Shula Sun's record entered the Gallup chart at No.118.

The following week it went up to 90. Radio One playlisted it.

On March 3rd it appeared for the first time in Music Week's Top 75 at No. 74. The promotion department of Trolfid Records sent out further 12-inch copies to all radio stations followed up by visits from the regional men exhorting the various producers and disc jockeys to keep up with the record.

Contact was made with the American office of the company and it was arranged that Shula Sun should fly to Britain for a five-day promotional tour. A video film of the artiste performing the song was made in readiness for insertion in Top of the Pops.

The tour was fixed for March 9th to 13th.

Trolfid's president, James Vaughan, contacted his friend Superintendent Cecil Page of Scotland Yard's Drugs Squad with the result that Detective Chief Inspector Knox alias Jeremy Rowlands was once again enlisted as tour manager.

This time he was more successful.

Chapter 13

'Hi,' said Robin Knox. He was in the Promotion Department of Trolfid Records talking to the red-haired girl he had last spoken to after Christmas. Her name was Ellen.

'Hi. Working for us again then?'

'Something like that. How's things?'

'Fine. Did you ever find that guy you were looking for, Richard?'

'Nope. Have you seen him since?'

'No. I reckon he must be spending the winter in the Canaries or something.' They both laughed and 'Jeremy Rowlands' picked up the itinerary with his name on it.

The first port of call, after picking his guests up early in the morning at Heathrow, was Liverpool. 'We have organised five days in the North,' explained James Vaughan. 'Cuts down on the travelling and there is heavy population density up there.'

Knox read the list. Manchester, Sheffield, Birmingham, Coventry and Leeds.

'Sunday is a free day. Get settled in because the first interview is on Radio City at eleven in the morning.'

Heathrow on Sunday was like Blackpool Central Station used to be at the start of the Wakes Week, before they invented cheap flights to Majorca.

Families of squealing children and harassed parents proliferated round the passenger terminals but Chief Inspector Knox still had no difficulty in picking out his charges. There was Frankie Lucerelli, Texas hat still perched atop his greasy black locks, now longer than collar length so that, from the back, he looked like a woman and Knox thought strangers might whistle at him in the street.

'Hi Jes,' he smiled, obviously pleased to see him. 'Boy, am I sick of toting her around. Jeez, man, since the record got to No.1 she has been too much. I tell you, she thinks she's another Diana Ross.'

Shula Sun flounced several paces behind him and was immediately pounced on by a cluster of small children with autograph books who recognised her from the adverts in their pop papers. It was not hard to distinguish her from other black singers. She was the only one given to wearing giant tangerine wigs with matching lipstick.

Knox took charge of the luggage and loaded it into the back of the Nissan Bluebird Estate hired for the tour. Lucerelli helped Shula Sun into the back seat. 'Put your feet up a little, baby,' he said. 'Let the asshole rot,' he whispered to Knox as he took his place alongside him at the front.

Shula Sun slept for most of the journey. They stopped for lunch at the Keele Service Station on the M6 where the two men had something to eat. 'I'd let her sleep on,' advised the American, shutting the car door quietly so as not to waken her. 'Someone might steal her.'

'She might be hungry later on,' pointed out Knox. 'You don't like her much, do you?'

'What? She treats us like dirt, man; ordering us around like we was her servants or something. She's only some back street, small town kid who got lucky. Give her another six months and she'll be back in the cotton fields or the assembly line at Ford's.'

'You're probably right,' agreed 'Jeremy Rowlands' and Shula Sun slept all the way to Liverpool.

They were booked into the St George's Hotel in the centre of the city, convenient for the visits the following day. After they had eaten dinner, Knox offered to drive them round the city to look at the sights, the Pier Head, the Liver Buildings, the Cavern site. But Shula Sun wasn't interested.

'Cities are like clubs,' she said. 'Seen one, you've seen them all. I just want to stay here and rest.'

'How can you say all cities look alike?' argued Knox, forgetting his designated role as menial. 'That's just ridiculous.' Lucerelli looked up from his second helping of Black Forest Gateau, sensing a fight brewing.

'They're just a collection of buildings.'

'It's not just the buildings. It's the people, the atmosphere, the different lifestyles. . .'

'For God's sake,' she screamed, causing a bordering diner to choke on his crème caramel. 'Will you shut up? You're annoying me. You're ruining my vibes. I just want to be allowed to get on with my career and you're supposed to be helping me. If you wanna go sightseeing, you go. I'll get the record company to send someone else to drive me around; someone who is interested in furthering my ongoing musical situation.' She banged down her wine glass and stormed out of the restaurant leaving Knox speechless.

'All you can expect from her,' commented Lucerelli. 'Like I say, give her six months.'

'It just annoys me that somebody like that should get the chance of all this foreign travel and be so unappreciative.'

The American shrugged. 'So what. Listen, you and me will go out tonight and find some pussy in this bad old city.'

Knox, remembering Nottingham, did not care to imagine what type of 'pussy' Lucerelli might find but he went along anyway. This was his big chance to find out more about the cocaine set-up and possibly discover what had happened to Richard Marchant.

They started out at the Grapes in Matthew Street and ended up three hours and six pubs later in the Yankee Clipper Club in Temple Street. Knox thought that his father-in-law would have been better suited to the job, Glass's capacity for drink being legendary at the Yard.

'I'm pissed,' Lucerelli informed him, sinking into a basement bench.

There might not be a better moment. 'Have you any coke on you?' asked Knox innocently, setting down two drinks on the table.

'Give me a chance, man. I've only been here twelve hours. I should have some tomorrow though.'

'Really? That was quick work. Not Richard Marchant again?'

'Yep.'

'I wondered what had happened to him. He was supposed to meet me over Christmas with some stuff, you may remember?'

'Huh.' Lucerelli showed little interest. 'Really?'

'How did you get hold of him?'

'He gave me his phone number last trip.' Knox said nothing but he remembered that the American had given the impression at the time that he had no knowledge of Marchant's whereabouts. Was Lucerelli part of the network?

'Where does he live?' he asked casually.

'I don't know. Somewhere in the country I think. The phone number was all figures.'

'He's coming up to Liverpool then is he?'

'First thing in the morning.'

'Maybe he'll get me some.'

'Yeah, why not? Say, drink up and I'll get them in. It sure is quiet in here.' Knox looked around. Only a dozen people sat in the dimly lit interior. Two girls in long skirts danced to the jukebox for a time but eventually surrendered to the tedium of the evening and sat down again.

'Personally,' said Knox, 'I'm ready for bed.' He did not like the look of either of the girls, one of whom could have doubled for Bela Lugosi. 'It has been a long day and we have an early start in the morning.'

'Yeah, maybe you're right,' capitulated the other. 'We might see something on the way back to the hotel.' But the only encounters they had were with rowdy, drunken yobs in the streets outside the club, many of them girls.

Richard Marchant kept his appointment the next morning, arriving as they were leaving the restaurant after breakfast.

'What happened to you on Boxing Day?' asked Knox.

Marchant casually murmured something about getting held up, made no apology and obviously considered the matter closed, going off with Lucerelli to discuss their business in the privacy of the American's room. When they returned, Knox tried again.

'I still have the money. Can you get me some coke or not?'

Marchant's expression was contemptuous. 'It will cost you a grand. No small orders in future.'

'The cash is no problem. Just tell me where and when.'

'All right. Where will you be this week?'

Knox went over the itinerary. 'As soon as possible,' he said.

'How about Birmingham on Thursday?'

'Okay.'

'I don't suppose there's any chance of making it to Stratford is there? It would be better for me.'

Knox consulted his list. The regional promotion men usually took Shula out in the daytimes so he would be free. 'About lunchtime?' he suggested. Stratford was only a half hour drive from Birmingham.

'In the Moat House Hotel. Don't forget the money.'

'I won't.' He turned to Lucerelli. 'Is Shula coming down? We have to meet Dicky Sterling in five minutes.'

'Who's he?'

'The Northern promotion guy. He's taking you to the radio station. The Radio Merseyside interview's at eleven.'

'I must be leaving,' interrupted Marchant. 'See you on Thursday.' He marched out of the foyer, swinging his brown case, still wearing denims and shoulder length hair.

'Who's doing the interview at Merseyside?'

'Billy Butler. You'll love him. Biggest listening figures in the city. They say he speaks broad Scouse, that's the local dialect. She won't understand a word he says so he'll just take the piss out of her.'

'I like it,' chortled Lucerelli. 'Who's after that?'

'A quick drink at the Eagle down the road then off to the hotel in Southport. A picturesque resort just up the coast,' he added for the benefit of Shula Sun who had just joined them, but she ignored the jibe.

She showed equal lack of interest some hours later when they were driving down the tree-lined boulevard of Lord Street, sitting in the back seat of the car pretending to be asleep.

'What did you do before this?' asked Knox, determined to make her talk.

'He means before you became a superstar,' added Lucerelli sarcastically.

'Oh, I didn't have a job, I was on Welfare. I had a baby when I was in High School so I just picked up a cheque every week.'

Knox couldn't resist it. 'He's married now is he, your son?'

'Are you joking?' she flared. 'He's a baby. How old do you think I am? I have him fostered out. He's OK.'

'Do you ever see him?'

'Listen honey, I ain't been near that city since I left. I've been far too busy, you know. My public wants to see me. Maybe when I've been touring a while longer I'll go back but not yet.'

Nice family girl, thought Knox and realised how he was missing his Sue.

'Hey, Jes, is there food at this hotel?'

'Excellent food Frankie,' they were booked into the Prince of Wales on Lord Street, 'but not much time to eat it. We leave for Tiffany's at eight and it's six-thirty now.'

'Always time to eat.' The cocaine had put him in good humour.

'It must be your lucky night then because the last club we go to has a big buffet on tonight.'

They visited three clubs and landed back at the hotel at three. Knox was up at eight. He bought a copy of The Megaphone which he took into the restaurant with him and started reading the back page over his cereal.

Oddly enough, at Scotland Yard, Detective Chief Inspector Glass was reading the very same thing.

'What do you fancy for the Champion Hurdle then?' asked Glass. It was the first day of the Cheltenham Spring Meeting. 'I see The Hunter has napped Captain Jonathan.'

'This canteen gets worse,' remarked Sergeant Evans. 'Just look at the state of this egg. You could play cricket with it.'

'I reckon Deva will win.'

'Let's have a look,' said Evans, taking the paper from him. 'Hmmmm, Monksfield would have beaten any of these.'

'Have you done anything for the Gold Cup yet?'

'Sailor's Delight. It's the only one in it.'

'Even with Lord Crossens riding?'

'That horse would win with you riding. Anyway, he won two National trials up North.'

'Yes but he will be riding against professionals here.' He lit his sixth Craven A of the morning. 'I believe Knox has gone off on this drugs thing again. Have you heard from him?'

'Not yet, have you?'

'No. I haven't been round to Sue's this week. Too much on. I wouldn't mind taking a day off on Thursday though, go to the Gold Cup. Do you fancy it?'

'Do you know, I wouldn't mind, if I can get the leave.'

'Let me know then.' He groaned. 'And now back to that bloody paperwork. I can tell you, they are turning the force into another civil service. It's all right for young Knox, sunning himself round the country. What a life!'

Actually, Detective Chief Inspector Knox was getting little chance to enjoy the mild spring weather. The first appointment of the day was forty miles away in Manchester at eleven o'clock. Despite the building of the M62 from Liverpool to Manchester, the old East Lancashire Road was still clogged up with big diesel lorries pouring black noxious fumes over the surrounding industrial wasteland which meant he was hard pressed to get there on time.

'What is this show?' asked Lucerelli, not in a good humour because he had missed his breakfast.

'A film spot for 'Live on Two' which goes out tomorrow.'

Lucerelli's temper improved when he saw the selection of food available at Granada's Festival Café and, while Shula Sun was in the studio, he ate his way steadily through the menu.

Shooting was finished by mid-afternoon. 'I'll lead the way back to the hotel,' said Dicky Sterling, hopping from foot to foot like a sparrow with St Vitus's Dance. 'Just in time to drop off your bags then we have interviews at Piccadilly and Radio Manchester. We mustn't be late.'

Lucerelli, however, insisted on delaying matters long enough to have a quick snack in the hotel coffee shop, an eating house shaped like a Polo mint with stools round the outside and waitresses serving from the middle.

Knox looked at his watch. Five o'clock. Two more radio interviews then three late night discos with dinner in between. No wonder pop stars were well paid.

'Black coffee,' he told the waitress. 'Help keep me awake.'

A telephone call a few minutes later did nothing to dispel his gloom. The record company rang to tell him that Shula Sun's record had gone up to No.37 in the charts and she was wanted in London the next day to record a spot on Top of the Pops.

'You should be finished for five. Where are you at night?'

'Sheffield,' groaned Knox. He broke the news to Lucerelli.

'Up at dawn I'm afraid,' he said.

'So what, man?' replied the other unconcernedly. 'You can't eat, drink or do anything while you're asleep so you ain't missing nothin'.'

'I suppose not.' He was not keen on this undercover work. He preferred more active police work, questioning suspects, visiting the scenes of crimes, looking for miscreants. Instead he was poncing about the country dressed up like a rock'n'roll singer and hardly a sniff at a villain in weeks. 'And it's good getting Top of the Pops isn't it?' he said, anxious to show some enthusiasm.

'I thought they had a video,' said Dicky Sterling.

'Apparently, as she was in the country they thought they would use her live.'

Knox allowed Dicky Sterling to take Shula Sun round the radio stations whilst he stayed at the hotel to make his phone calls. Sergeant Evans was not in but he was able to get hold of Sue. He recounted the events to date.

Three clubs were scheduled for the evening but his ambitions to be back in the hotel for one a.m. were quickly thwarted. The first club had five discos connected by a maze of passages and stairways and Shula insisted on performing in every one. Then, at Heriots, he got into an altercation with a youth with spiky orange hair who belonged in the next room where they were playing punk rock. By the time they reached the last venue, they were running an hour late and Knox was falling asleep.

'What time does this place close?' asked the singer.

'Two, miss,' replied the doorman who was young enough to be in awe of pop stars.

'Oh good. Time to stay for a boogie.'

Knox groaned. He was getting too old for the playboy life. Was it only five years ago he would stay all night at Tramps?

It was three when they eventually returned to the Piccadilly Hotel and five when they set off for London, barely time for him to drink his Ovaltine.

The recording for Top of the Pops went well. Backing tracks from the record were used behind Shula's voice and the expertise of the sound engineers made sure her contribution was a passable impersonation of the original. Lucerelli and Knox watched her between snacks in the canteen.

'They must be good those guys,' said Lucerelli. 'It took her sixty-five takes before she got it right on the original.'

'No time to stop for food,' said Knox as they ran to the car for the journey back North. 'Sheffield next stop. Another two hundred miles.'

They made it with ten minutes to spare. Knox drove straight to the first PA where the manager responded to Lucerelli's lamentations of starvation and provided hamburgers, chicken in the basket and scampi that followed each other down his throat in quick succession, washed down by cheap sparkling wine.

'Right, I'm fixed up for the night, now where's next? I'm on my way, baby.' The wine after the cannabis smoked in the car was beginning to take effect. Knox hoped no more orgies would be set up like the one in Nottingham.

He was lucky. By midnight, Lucerelli's exhilaration had turned to torpor, Shula Sun was complaining of a sore throat ('To a singer that is like gangrene to an athlete') and Knox was able to get them back to the hotel for two.

He wanted to be fresh for the next day, the day of the long awaited meeting with Richard Marchant.

It was also an important day for Detective Chief Inspector Glass. Much more important than he realised when he decided to go to Cheltenham for the Gold Cup.

Chapter 14

The Hunter's selection was given a middle page spread in The Megaphone.

THREE IN A ROW FOR LADY VERONICA
Having already justified my faith by winning the Hennessy Cognac Gold Cup and the King George VI Chase, I have little doubt that Lady Veronica will take the coveted Gold Cup at Cheltenham this afternoon. Although last year's winner, Sailor's Delight, will be hoping to be the first horse since L'Escargot in 1970-71 to take the trophy two years running, I fancy that inexperienced owner-jockey Lord Crossens will have his eye too much on the Grand National for which Sailor's Delight is also favourite.

Detective Chief Inspector Glass read the article as he took breakfast in his attic flat in Shepherd's Bush.

'Sticking his neck out there,' he murmured to his cat, Sailor, a large white creature with grey patches and a bushy tail. 'Surely he wouldn't try it again if he was guilty; and if he wasn't he can't expect to be lucky a third time with Lady Veronica.' Sailor Glass nodded wisely and washed behind his right ear with his paw.

Neither do I hold out much hope for Sailor's Delight's stable companion,
Little Sweetheart, after her rather disappointing showing in the King George VI Chase on Boxing Day, notwithsatnding the subsequent suspension of her jockey, John Haile. She was also a

good length behind The Punter when coming second in the recent Leopardstown Chase.

'And would have come first if Willie Leigh had been riding,' thought Glass angrily. He had lost £2 on that race.

He was journeying to Cheltenham alone, Sergeant Evans having sent word to say that he was involved in an embassy siege and could not get away.

The fine sunny weather prompted him to discard his greatcoat in favour of an oversize hacking jacket; cavalry twill slacks and a brown trilby that, atop its previous owner, had seen service in World War Two. Indeed, weathermen proudly proclaimed it was the warmest March since 1917 as if they had been instrumental in producing it.

Before leaving he rang Albert Beaton and invited himself for drinks in the trainer's tent on the course.

'Don't forget to back the winner,' Bertie told him.

'Which one will it be?'

'Sailor's Delight of course. Barring accidents.' The last sentence was spoken grimly.

'I'll risk a bluey on him,' said Glass. Surely there would not be another attempt to stop Bertie Beaton's horses. Perhaps he ought to have investigated more intensively though he did not know how.

He set off in the Mini Countryman and took the M40 Oxford road which he reached in little over an hour. Having time in hand, he decided to make a slight detour and call on some friends in Stratford on Avon.

It was a decision that would have far-reaching effects.

He drove along the A34, through the village of Woodstock by Blenheim Palace. It was one of his favourite spots. The teashops, white painted pubs and souvenir shops overrun with tourists contrasted with the timeless magnificence of the mansion behind the stone walls.

At Tredington he switched to the A422 Banbury road into Stratford, his friends living off this road in the plush residential area just outside the town.

When he arrived, however, they were out. Probably at the theatre, he conjectured, because both of them worked for the Royal Shakespeare Company.

He decided to go to the Moat House Hotel for a drink and a bite to eat. He chose the Moat House because it was nearby and he would not have to negotiate the town centre traffic, Stratford not being short of visitors during the Cheltenham Spring Meeting.

It was the worst choice he could have made.

He went into the Tavern Restaurant where they were offering a selection of hot and cold buffets. It was crowded and Glass suspected that many of those present would be found at Cheltenham later in the afternoon. He pushed his way to the bar and ordered a Southern Comfort.

'Detective Chief Inspector Glass, isn't it?' The tall, well-groomed man next to him held out his hand. 'Jeffrey Leek-Turner, Jockey Club. We met over that John Haile business.' He was approaching sixty but his erect bearing and smooth skin made him look ten years younger and the silver hair, parted at the side, showed no signs of receding. Glass thought he had probably served in the Guards.

They shook hands. 'Let me get you a drink,' offered the policeman.

'Very civil of you. I'll have a whisky.'

He ordered the drink and looked around. All the seats were taken. 'Busy today,' he commented.

'Most of them are here for the meeting. Are you going yourself, Inspector?' he eyed Glass's apparel curiously, 'or are you here on business?'

'No, just a day out at the races.' He took out a Craven A and held out the packet.

'Not for me thanks. I stick to the pipe.'

'What happened to John Haile in the end?'

'Investigation still going on. Have your people dropped it?'

'Not dropped it exactly.' He lit his cigarette and flicked the match into the ashtray on the counter. 'The file is still open but more cases came in and we reached a dead end with that one. Lack of evidence.'

'Yes, the same with us. We had a private chap on it, Hallé.'

'Harry who?'

'Not Harry, Hallé. After the orchestra.'

'Oh yes,' smiled Glass weakly. He had as little time for private detectives as he had for the graduates from the police college.

'The thing is, has he got anywhere with it?'

'He has asked a lot of questions, interviewed all the trainers and owners involved in the two races concerned but, no, nothing new has come up.'

'How long was John Haile suspended?'

'Three months. He'll be back in time for the Grand National, that's if anyone will want to use him again.'

'So we're all back where we started from then?'

'It appears that way. Our man reckons some sort of syndicate fraud could have been perpetrated at the King George.'

'What about the Hennessy?'

'We're prepared to accept it was a genuine accident. You know Leigh has not raced since? They say he's lost his nerve, all that was a cover up.'

'Really? But even if we disregard him, we still have somebody phoning John Haile to throw a race because they stand to win money if Sailor's Delight loses.' He thought of Dermot Draper, the bookmaker. 'Or lose money if it wins.'

'Yes, but the only so-called evidence we have is that one solitary call. Suppose that call never happened and Haile, like Leigh, was just making an excuse for his bad riding. Then there would be no case at all.' He pointed to the detective's empty glass

'Another of those?'

'Why not?'

Glass was not happy with the way the Jockey Club seemed to be handling the case. A typical example of sweeping things under the carpet, he thought, pretending they had never happened. No case at all, indeed. Nicola Beaton would not like that.

He glanced round the crowded bar and his eye caught a man he thought he recognised standing at the door. He wore a sweatshirt bearing the emblem of New York University and a pair of red denim jeans. He was carrying a canvas shoulder bag inscribed Trolfid Records.

'Excuse me a moment,' he said and hurried over to the door.

'Whatever are you doing here?' he asked Detective Chief Inspector Knox.

Breakfast was taken early at the Grosvenor House Hotel, Sheffield.

It took seven room calls to bring Shula Sun to the table for seven-thirty but she finally made it, resplendent in blue frizzy wig with matching nail polish. Dark suited sales representatives peering from behind their Daily Telegraphs gaped at the sight, allowing thin marmalade to run down their freshly-shaven chins.

Whilst she picked at her roll and coffee, Frankie Lucerelli ate two fried breakfasts and Robin Knox enjoyed a bowl of All Bran and read The Megaphone. On the sports page, promoted to a middle section pull-out, The Hunter had remained faithful to his favourite horse. *'THREE IN A ROW FOR LADY VERONICA'* read the headline.

'OK, man. Ready to go.' Lucerelli wiped the recalcitrant trickles of fat from his lips and pushed away the greasy plates.

'I ain't finished my roll,' objected Shula Sun.

'Well take it with you. We ain't got all day.'

By eight-thirty they were speeding down the M1. Knox took the motorway route all the way, picking up the M69 at Leicester and going in on the M6 and M38, right into the city centre of Birmingham.

The Trolfid Records Southern Promotion man, Vince Arrow, met them at the Midland Hotel in New Street. He was a slim man with thinning hair which he compensated for by growing long strands at the sides which dangled over his ears like ferns in a hanging basket.

118

'Hello Jeremy love, nice to meet you and Frankie isn't it? And Shula, darling, you're looking wonderful.' Shula Sun beamed and the two men cringed as limp handshakes for everyone followed with a wet kiss on Shula's cheek that missed its target and smudged her eye make-up. She gave a smile of annoyance and brushed it with her finger.

'Hey, this guy is a fruitcake, man,' hissed Lucerelli to Knox.

'Right then, if you dears want to change, I thought we would have a quick coffee in the lounge then get to the studio for about twelve. Jeremy, do you want to park your car in the multi-storey across the way?'

'What exactly is arranged for today?'

'I'm taking them to Pebble Mill now. Then, this afternoon, we have Beacon and Birmingham.'

'So you don't need me, right?' He got back in the car.

Vince Arrow looked surprised. 'I suppose not.'

'Good. I have some business to take care of so if you would like to grab hold of the luggage from the boot, I'll see you back at the hotel for dinner.'

He remained in the driving seat whilst Arrow struggled with the cases, watched with amusement by Lucerelli.

'Get some for me,' whispered Lucerelli, coming over to the car window and pushing some notes into Knox's hand. 'There's £150 there.'

'Right.' Knox drove round the back of the hotel, beneath the New Street Station complex and eventually back on the ring road to the A34 turn-off. The traffic was heavy up to the outskirts of Solihull but, once he had passed the M42 connection, the road was clear. He passed through Henley-in-Arden where the sun came out, shining on the half-timbered houses and budding trees. He was tempted to stop for a drink at one of the little teashops but he did not want to risk being late for Richard Marchant.

In fact he reached the Moat House with time to spare.

Casually he strolled into the hotel and stood at the door of the restaurant trying to spot his man in the crowd. He experienced the familiar tingle of excitement down his spine when a voice at his elbow suddenly said, 'Whatever are you doing here?' He looked quickly round.

'Good God,' he exclaimed. 'Whatever are you doing here?'

'I just said that,' said Glass.

'I'm supposed to be meeting Marchant here, the drug contact. The one that didn't turn up on Boxing Day.' He kept his voice a low murmur.

'What time is he due?'

'Twelve.'

'It's only quarter to. Could you risk a drink? I'm with this bloke from the Jockey Club, Leek-Turner.'

'Better not. I'm Jeremy Rowlands here, remember. Record promoter and cocaine addict.'

'You could always say I'm a friend of yours who drives lorries for British Rail.'

'In that outfit?' he peered at the large hacking jacket. 'I take it you're going to the races.'

'Day's leave. I thought I'd look in.'

'You do all right with your days' leave I must say.'

'Oh yes, I had one in February too. Jim Evans was going to come with me but he has got himself involved with one of those embassy sieges in

Kensington that seem to be popular nowadays. Arabs running all over the place firing rifles.'

'Arabs or Libyans?'

'I don't know. They all look the same to me. We should have sent them all back to the desert while we had the chance. Now they own half the country and tell us what we can show on our own television sets. Any day now they'll be giving us all notice to get out and we'll all have to move to Australia.'

'So that was why Evans was not in when I rang on Tuesday.'

'Probably. Was it anything important?'

'No. Only to tell him I was meeting Marchant today.' The need for secrecy asserted itself. 'And now you had better go. He might be early.'

'Best of luck then. When does this tour finish?'

'Tomorrow in Leeds.'

'I'll probably see you at the weekend then. I'll be round for Sunday dinner. Bring you a bottle of plonk out of my winnings.'

'See you then.' Glass walked back to the bar and Knox turned round to go out to the foyer. Almost bumping into Richard Marchant who had apparently been standing not a yard behind him. How much had he heard?

'Friend of yours?'

So Marchant had seen him talking to Glass. 'Not really. He drives a lorry for British Rail. Used to be a roadie years ago. That's where I knew him from.' He met the other's eyes. 'Have you got the stuff?'

Marchant tapped the pocket of his jeans.

'Come on out to my van.' The dealer led him out to the car park. He was wearing the same faded denims he had worn at Nottingham and again at Liverpool. If he was making much money as a delivery boy, thought Knox, it was certainly not being spent on clothes.

'Do you live in Stratford?' he asked.

Richard Marchant said nothing. He opened the sliding front door of his rusting transit van and from under the dashboard produced a flat brown packet the size of ten cigarettes. 'It's all there.'

The detective took it. 'A grand I believe you said?' He handed over the notes. 'And Frankie wondered if you could let me have some more for him.'

'How much?'

'He gave me a hundred and fifty.'

Marchant seemed to be having trouble making up his mind. 'I haven't got it here,' he said at last.

'When could you get it? This afternoon?'

Again the pause. 'Maybe.'

'Should I come with you?'

'No I'll bring it myself. Where are you tonight?'

Knox consulted his itinerary. 'We end up at the Elbow Room in Birmingham. Do you know it?'

'Yes. It's in Aston. Think of the Villa. Midnight?'

'Better make it one o'clock.' He allowed for Shula Sun's usual tardiness. 'Er, if I wanted more coke, a big quantity, could you get it?'

'What do you call big?'

'Say five grand.'

Richard Marchant's face remained impassive. 'Maybe.'

'You don't know?'

'I would have to ask.'

Knox became assertive. 'Why not take me to the guy you deal with? It would save time.'

'He might not want to see you. Like I say, I'll have to ask him.'

'Can I have my answer tonight?'

'Perhaps. What do you want five grand's worth for anyway?'

'That's my business.'

'Tonight then.' Marchant climbed into the driving seat, slid the door to after him and drove slowly out of the car park.

The detective was tempted to follow him but decided against it. Instead he took the small brown packet up to his own car and drove off up the A34 back to Birmingham.

He did not see the long-haired girl with the black leather jacket and faded denim jeans slip out of the hotel and watch him drive away. And he was a good mile away when the transit van reappeared, chugging noisily, and stopped by the car park entrance.

The girl ran towards it and jumped into the front passenger seat.

'Well?' said Richard Marchant.

'Yes,' replied the girl. 'He was a pig all right. I heard him talking to some old geezer about doping.'

'Dope?'

'No they was talking about horses, doping horses.'

'So. Our Jeremy Rowlands is not what he appears to be. I never did trust him. I wonder what my instructions will be on this one.' His hand went down to his side and he fingered the sharp blade of a knife. 'Taylor does not like traitors.'

'He must have been planted specially.'

'Yes.' He switched on the car radio. Shula Sun was singing 'Reminisce About The One You Miss'. 'In which case we must find out where he came from and send him back.' He rubbed his chin ruminatively. 'On the other hand, parcel post is so expensive nowadays. Maybe,' said Richard Marchant, 'we will just send his hands.'

'Sorry about that,' said Detective Chief Inspector Glass, returning to the bar. 'Fellow I used to know; drives a lorry for British Rail.'

'Your drink.' Leek-Turner handed across a Southern Comfort. 'Do you fancy something to eat? The crowd is thinning out a bit now, there are a few empty seats on that side.'

The two men commandeered a table and availed themselves of the cold buffet.

'So your investigation is virtually closed too then,' continued Glass, biting hungrily into a chicken leg.

'I prefer to say that we have found no evidence to indicate doping or, indeed, any foul play.' He moved his seat to let a long-haired girl pass by.

'Do you really?' Glass washed down a tough bit of wing with Southern Comfort. 'But what about Haile's story? Or the common denominators?'

'Common denominators?'

'Both horses were owned by Lord Crossens and both were trained by Albert Beaton.'

'Yes. Well we followed both those lines of enquiry but nothing emerged to suggest they were significant. As for Haile, our man did suspect some sort of fraud was in operation but there was nothing to support this theory other than the jockey's statement.'

'Would a jockey risk a three month ban just to cover up his inability to win a race?'

Leek-Turner was floundering. 'He may have said it on the spur of the moment. Frightened of the owner's wrath after losing.'

'But it was five days later that he told this story and then only after I had interrogated him.' But Glass knew he was wasting his time. It was going to be a 'whitewash' job. Nothing more would be heard. John Haile would ride again and all would be conveniently forgotten.

Until there was another 'accident'!

He pushed away his plate, full of chicken bones and skin, and rose to his feet. 'I must be going or I shall miss the first race. Can I offer you a lift?'

'No thanks, I have the Rolls outside.'

'Of course.' He wondered if his Mini Countryman would fit in the boot. 'I'll see you again, sir.'

'Let's hope not professionally,' smiled Mr.Leek-Turner.

But his hopes were dashed within hours.

Chapter 15

Cheltenham during the Spring Meeting has an atmosphere unlike any racecourse in the world. It might be argued that Royal Ascot is more fashionable or that the Grand National is a bigger legend but, from a racing point of view, Cheltenham represents the pinnacle of National Hunt racing when the cream of steeplechasers and hurdlers compete in such distinguished races as the Champion Hurdle, the Daily Express Triumph Hurdle, the Queen Elizabeth the Queen Mother Champion Steeplechase and, of course, the Gold Cup Steeplechase itself. Not even Epsom on Derby Day, the equivalent flat racing event, can match the thrills of the Spring Meeting.

Gate receipts were set for an all time record as spectators, encouraged by the delightful mild weather, poured into Cheltenham from all directions. The ground was firm, the going was good and all was set for an excellent day's racing in the presence of the Royal Family.

Detective Chief Inspector Glass parked his car in the public car park and walked the quarter of a mile to the chalet block where Bertie Beaton had his tent. The trainer was inside with his daughter.

'Lovely day,' he greeted them.

'A change from the last few years. We've become used to monsoons during Gold Cup Week.'

'What time is the first race?'

Bertie Beaton handed him a racecard. 'You will just catch it. We have nothing running until the Gold Cup.'

'Who is riding Little Sweetheart?' asked Glass. 'There was just a blank beside it in The Megaphone.'

'That's because John Haile was originally booked and now, of course, he cannot ride.'

'So. . . ?'

'Willie is riding her,' said Nicola Beaton quietly.

'Oh. He's better then?'

'He's been better for some time. He just preferred to make his return without any fuss.'

'What did the owner have to say about that?'

'We have not actually told him. He's been too busy with Sailor's Delight which he's riding himself. He thinks no other horse has a chance.'

'And has it?'

Nicola smiled. 'Sailor's Delight could win that race with a chimpanzee on his back. With Lord Crossens, I'm not so sure.'

'Is Willie upset that he's not riding the favourite?'

'Not really. He's hoping he can beat Lord Crossens just to show him he isn't the fool he takes him for.'

'No chance,' chimed Bertie. 'It's a walkover.'

Glass remembered Bertie's earlier warning on the telephone. 'You're not expecting any sort of trouble are you? No warnings or anything?'

'No, Walter. Nothing at all. Let's face it, we've had dozens of horses running since Boxing Day and nothing untoward has occurred.'

'Let's hope it stays that way.' He did not mention Leek-Turner's abdication of responsibility which he guessed would rouse Nicola to a new fury. 'I'd better go and put my money on.'

'Don't forget to put something on Willie. Each way.' For the first time he detected a sign of gentleness and concern behind Nicola's confident front. He realised the encouragement and determination she must have needed to get her boyfriend back in the saddle.

'Don't worry. I'll have a fiver on him as well. I'll see you later for the champagne.'

He left the chalets for the Members' Enclosure, stopping on the way to place his bets.

He could only get 8-11 on Sailor's Delight and the latest forecast on the others was 3-1 The Punter (after his storming finish in the King George and his win at Leopardstown). 7-2 Lady Veronica, 5-1 Reverend Shaker (recent winner of the Massey Ferguson Gold Cup and the only American entry which meant all the tourists' money would be on it) and 13-2 Little Sweetheart (not expected to last the distance). There were eighteen runners in all but the rest were outsiders according to the bookmakers and Glass never backed outsiders.

He was in time to see the finish of the first race, the Daily Express Triumph Hurdle, but the result meant nothing to him. He went into the New Grandstand and had a drink in the Cottage Rake bar before returning to his spec for the second race, a steeplechase for amateur riders. This time he had remembered to bring his bulky ex-Navy binoculars and they bounced painfully against his hacking jacket as he walked.

After a few minutes, he got bored. It was like watching a football match where it was always half-time. Five minutes racing then half an hour's standing around. He decided to go to the Parade Ring to be sure of seeing the Gold Cup runners when they came out.

His large frame rested uncertainly on the tiny fixed stools but it was better than leaning over the shoulders of the mass of people who crammed the rails and pressed him from all sides as the first horses came through.

His view was unimpaired and it was not hard to spot Sailor's Delight, led out by a pretty stable girl, the smallest horse in the ring but certainly the best turned out. His black coat gleamed in the spring sunshine and his ears were pricked and alert. Following him round the ring was his stable companion, Little Sweetheart, chestnut and two hands higher.

The jockeys came out of the weighing room, through the pre-parade ring and towards the horses. Trainers and owners stood in groups. Nicola Beaton was talking to Willie Leigh whose appearance had set the crowd buzzing. Lord Crossens was listening impatiently to last minute advice from Bertie.

One by one the jockeys mounted and walked their horses out to the parade past the stands. Glass joined the stampede back to the Members' Enclosure to secure his view of the course.

A few minutes after three-thirty the starter's flag was raised and the Cheltenham Gold Cup was under way. As the horses flashed past the stands on their first circuit Little Sweetheart led the field, as was her wont, closely followed by a cluster of other horses, then a gap before Sailor's Delight.

The detective was able to follow the field out into the country thanks to the admirable magnification of his ex-Navy binoculars, although nothing of any note took place on that first circuit as the runners continued in virtually unchanging order. He had given up trying to distinguish one from the other, relying on the commentator who told him over the public address system that Reverend Shaker was closely behind Willie Leigh on Little Sweetheart followed by Lady Veronica (yes, he could pick out the grey), Hot California Nights (wasn't that the idiot that could not race a milkman's cart?) and The Punter. They were going away from him now for the second time and he thought he could see a blur of black indicating Sailor's Delight, still in the middle of the field.

Around him a party of raucous Irishmen, rotten with drink, were shouting for Lady Veronica with the same exhilaration that had kept the other residents of the Queen's Hotel in Cheltenham awake for the past three nights. Not to be outdone, nearby American tourists with Dak clothing and premature suntans were equally vocal in their encouragement for Reverend Shaker. There were no similar shouts from groups of Englishmen and Glass wondered what had happened to patriotism.

He adjusted his binoculars as the horse came to the water jump. Although ageing and somewhat shabby, their extremely powerful lenses probably afforded him a better view than anyone round him of the incident at that obstacle.

What he saw was the third horse (which it was he could not say) stumble as it approached the fence and the jockey fell into the path of the fifteen pursuant horses. He saw St..John's Ambulance men bring a stretcher out of their van and lift the injured man on to it. He saw another man, possibly a doctor, drive up in a saloon car and run across to examine the man on the stretcher. He could not see the expression on their faces but he could sense some urgency about the way they moved. And he could see, as they loaded the stretcher into the back of the ambulance, that the blanket was drawn up to COVER THE JOCKEY'S HEAD.

Peter Bromley took up the commentary three fences from home.

'And it's still Little Sweetheart who has led this field from the start but now Sailor's Delight is moving forward on one of his familiar runs to challenge and Lady Veronica and The Punter are right behind as they come down the hill to the third fence.

And they are all safely over, just two fences to go in the Gold Cup and now Sailor's Delight, the favourite, takes the lead as his stable companion Little Sweetheart drops back and The Punter moves into second place followed by Lady Veronica the grey for Ireland and I can hear the cheers from the Irish contingent here today but it's still Sailor's Delight, remember he won this race by twenty lengths last year, moving away from the others and he jumps the second last but, oh dear, he jumped that badly.

He's still on his feet but The Punter has taken up the lead with Ray Allan urging him on as they round the home turn to the last fence and it's between these two now with Little Sweetheart, Lady Veronica some two lengths behind and behind them Northern Soul and Briarwood. And as they come to the last fence it's Sailor's Delight, the favourite, and The Punter, neck and neck oh, and another blunder there by Sailor's Delight, Lord Crossens his owner is holding on in the saddle but The Punter jumped that superbly and he's now a good length clear as they race up the hill to the finish here at Cheltenham and The Punter is holding off the challenge and it's going to be The Punter, owned by Mrs.Peggy Bolton, trained by Ernie Coar and ridden by Ray Allan who has won the Gold Cup with Sailor's Delight second and a photo for third between Lady Veronica and Little Sweetheart.

Detective Chief Inspector Knox drove slowly back to Birmingham from Stratford, glad of a few hours to himself. For the first time in the case he felt that he was getting somewhere. His bait had been cast, tonight he would know if it had been taken.

He parked his car in the shoppers' car park behind the hotel and went up to his room, stopping to order tea and sandwiches from the hall porter. He stretched out on the bed. It was true what they said about slowing down at thirty. Once he would have taken the late nights in his stride but not now. He switched on the colour TV and was in time to see the start of the Gold Cup. Odd how both cases had dragged on so long, no real evidence, hardly cases at all. He could not see Glass in the crowds. He hoped that Marchant had not recognised Glass as a policeman; if he had there could be trouble. How ironic meeting like that just at the moment Marchant arrived.

The race began. The Willie Leigh affair seemed to have petered out, he never did think there was anything in it. He was surprised Glass had taken so much notice. Nicola Beaton's influence probably.

He saw Reverend Shaker fall, or rather he saw Thom Snaipe hurtle to the ground and the TV cameras lingered long enough to catch the killing blows to his skull by at least two metal horseshoes. Then the announcement after the race confirming that the jockey had been killed and Knox began to wonder all over again if Glass's intuition had been right all along. Perhaps there was a case after all.

His tea and sandwiches arrived, ham with cress, tomato and lettuce on wholemeal bread. He ate hungrily, his first meal since breakfast. Shula Sun was due back at five, time for a bath and maybe a quick nap and then another non-stop night except this time a promise of something at the end of it, a lead towards the cocaine dealers.

Shula Sun and entourage turned up on time from their tour of the radio stations, accompanied by Sandy Heneghan, still twitching and scurrying about like a hen that had mislaid its eggs. His colleague, Vince Arrow, was delighted with the day's proceedings. 'Lovely interviews, darling. You were wonderful.' Shula Sun beamed in full agreement and guests passing through reception stared at her tangerine wig.

Lucerelli removed his hat and wiped the top layer of sweat from his hair with the back of his hand. He then replaced the hat and repeated the action on his moustache. 'What's on tonight, man?'

'Three clubs here, in Coventry. Only a few miles away,' he added.

The American lit a joint and inhaled deeply. 'Did you get any coke for me?' he asked Knox openly.

'He's bringing it to the Elbow Room tonight, the last club we go to. He had no more on him but you can use some of mine if you want.'

'Fine.' Lucerelli held out his hand and the policeman handed across the flat packet from within his shoulder bag. 'Just time for a snort before dinner.'

Both promotion men joined them for the evening's PA's. The Coventry venue was another dance hall with under age drinkers who hurled abuse at the singer when she climbed onto the stage.

'Disco music is out now,' explained the bow-tied manager. 'It's all this electronic stuff here.'

'Say, look at that, they are ripping up the vouchers,' laughed Lucerelli, 'and throwing them at the old bag.' As fast as Vince Arrow and Sandy Heneghan passed out the 50p off leaflets, the kids tore them up until one enterprising Borstal prospect snatched the whole lot from Heneghan's trembling hands and, with a throw of superb accuracy, knocked Shula Sun's wig forward onto her mouth. The record played on as she fought to extract hair from her lips whilst keeping in time with the words.

'You can hardly call it a race riot,' murmured the manager. 'Most of the kids are blacker than she is. No discrimination there.'

'Look at them,' shouted Lucerelli, jumping up and down in excitement. 'Go on, more, more.' He waved his hat in the air wildly inciting the youths to further riots.

'I think we'd better get out,' said Knox, fearing for Shula Sun's safety. 'Get hold of a couple of your bouncers,' he instructed the manager. 'Frankie, get Shula off that stage.'

The first blow was struck as Lucerelli lifted Shula Sun bodily from the microphone, a Midland Red bus conductor breaking the nose of a five foot six mod from Wallsgrove wearing a Madonna T-shirt.

'The back doors,' panted the manager, aware that a major skirmish was imminent. 'Behind the dressing rooms. You can bring your car round the side.'

'I hope there will not be any more clubs like that,' said Shula Sun angrily as they finally drove away. Sandy Heneghan cringed apologetically but he had no need to worry. The next two venues, both in Birmingham, were sophisticated night spots catering for the second city élite, featuring plush décors, extravagant lighting systems, quiet restaurants and scantily dressed waitresses. The clientele consisted mainly of rich middle-aged businessmen and young, look-alike dolly birds.

'Nice place isn't it?' commented Sandy Heneghan, joining Knox at the bar at the second club. 'That light over the stage cost seven thousand you know.'

'Really?' The policeman thought nostalgically of his bachelor days spent in similar establishments.

'Oh yes. There is over a quarter of a million gone into this place. Look, if you hang on here, I'll go and organise some bubbly. The Manager is a personal friend of mine so we should be OK for a couple of bottles.'

'Yeah.' Sandy Heneghan seemed to be a personal friend of everyone. Indeed, he had virtually made a career out of it.

A polite trickle of applause signalled the end of Shula Sun's song. No vouchers were given out, nobody queued for autographs. This was not a record buying audience. Knox suspected that their visit had been arranged only because Heneghan owed the manager a few favours, probably his free admission to the club for the rest of the year. With promotion men it was always wheels within wheels.

They managed three bottles of the bubbly before Vince Arrow moved uncertainly to his feet. 'I think we had better be moving on to the Elbow

Room dears.' Knox looked across at Lucerelli, busy munching a beef burger he had cadged from the chef.

This was it. Would Marchant turn up this time? Or would Mr.Big himself come? Perhaps they would take him to their HQ. He would soon know.

The American winked wordlessly and brought his right thumb and index finger to his nose, a piece of mime Knox interpreted as an allusion to the forthcoming cocaine deal.

'Yes, let's be moving,' said Knox. They were already running late. Would Richard Marchant wait, that is if he turned up at all? He remembered his fruitless wait on Boxing Day in this same city.

The Elbow Room Club was a good three miles away across the city in the suburb of Aston, famous for its University and the Aston Villa football club.

'Good venue this,' remarked Vince Arrow. 'Lots of the bands come along here when they're gigging in town.'

Knox parked the car and they made their way up the steps to the club. It was well named as there was scarcely room to stand but Knox could not spot Richard Marchant among the crowd.

'Looks as if we're going to be disappointed,' said Lucerelli who had been looking for him too. 'That guy just ain't reliable.'

Another dead end, thought Knox. Back to square one. He was fed up with the case. Like Glass's, it seemed to get nowhere. Then. . . .

'Hey, there he is, in the corner behind the disco.' And there he was, still in his faded denims and talking to two men in white suits who would not have looked out of place in the East End.

'Who's the heavies?'

'I dunno. Ain't seen them before.' He walked across followed by the detective. 'Hey, Richie.' Marchant looked up. 'You got the stuff, man?'

Knox noticed a glance pass between Marchant and his minders. 'Certainly, have you got the money, Frankie?'

'I have it,' said Knox, pulling the notes from the pocket of his jeans. 'A hundred and fifty I believe.'

Marchant took the money without a word and handed a flat package to Lucerelli.

'Great,' said the American. He stuffed it down the waist band of his jeans. 'You coming for something to eat, Jes? I thought I saw a little cafe downstairs.'

'In a minute,' replied Knox. He looked inquiringly at Marchant who responded immediately.

'I have something for you in the van, Jes.' He smiled. 'Do you want to come down now, then we can take off?'

Suddenly, Knox felt something was wrong. The men with Marchant; what were they doing there? He looked around. Lucerelli had disappeared. Shula Sun was on the DJ's rostrum, belting out her song. Was Lucerelli in it too? Had they found out he was a detective?

He forced himself to smile back. 'Great. I'll follow you down.' But the two minders stayed behind him all the way.

They reached the street and Richard Marchant led the way to the transit van parked a hundred yards up the road. He opened the sliding doors on the passenger side and stood aside. 'Get in,' he instructed.

Knox stooped to climb into the front seat but his feet never left the ground.

'I hope you didn't hit him too hard, Rodney,' said Richard Marchant. 'Those new crowbars are not as strong as the old sort. We don't want to break them.' He looked down at the recumbent body of the policeman. 'Give him a hand to put him in the back, Lionel. And then let's get the hell away from here.'

He drove out of Birmingham on the Stratford road and Knox was still unconscious when they reached their destination.

Chapter 16

Detective Chief Inspector Glass went back to the Beatons' house after the day's racing and joined the family for dinner in the low beamed lounge.

'Two horses in the first three of the Gold Cup. Can't be bad.'

Nicola Beaton remained unconvinced. 'Sailor's Delight would easily have won if Willie had been riding. Did you see the mess Lord Crossens made of the last two fences?'

'I missed the end. I was watching what was happening at the Water Jump through my binoculars.'

'Terrible business,' said Bertie Beaton, shaking his head. 'That lad would have been champion jockey one day. More port, Walter?'

The policeman allowed his glass to be filled.

'There was nothing suspicious about the accident was there?' asked Nicola sharply.

'If there was, I haven't heard anything,' said Glass truthfully. But inside his instincts were screaming out that something was wrong. 'The lad was just unlucky that the horses following could not avoid him.'

Willie Leigh shuddered. 'And I was lucky.'

'Willie is coming into the business at the end of the season,' announced Bertie and Glass was heartened to see the pride and delight on his old friend's face. 'Keeping it in the family.'

'There is one race I want to win first,' said the jockey. 'If I can persuade the owner to let me ride Sailor's Delight, I know I can do it. The Grand National.'

'After the cock-up he made today, he would be a fool to stop you,' said Glass. 'By rights, he should have been half a mile in front of Little Sweetheart.'

Bertie Beaton rose to switch on the television ('a racing documentary on at eight o'clock') but he was early and in time to catch the end of Top of the Pops. Shula Sun's video of 'Reminisce About The One You Miss' was on.

'So that's what she looks like,' said Glass. 'Robin wasn't exaggerating after all. Christ Almighty. What a sight!' He turned to the others. 'My son-in-law is ferrying THAT around the country at the moment. Just look at that bloody orange hair.'

'Ah, so that is why he was dressed like that at Nottingham. Undercover work.' Nicola laughed. 'What exactly is he after?'

'Drugs. As a matter of fact, I saw him today, in the Stratford Moat House.'

'Mmmmm. They move in high circles these criminals. Must be more money in it than training horses. And what is she like this woman?'

'A pain in the backside from what I gather.' They laughed and the discussion moved on.

'You are enjoying your racing again then, Bertie?' said Glass sometime later.

'I reckon so. Willie back in the saddle helped, eh Nikki?'

Nicola Beaton smiled. 'It seems like our troubles are over,' she admitted.

The remark was premature. By the next night, not a trainer in England felt safe letting his horses out of their stables.

Chapter 17

'The Arabs didn't get you then?' It was Friday morning in the Scotland Yard canteen and Detective Chief Inspector Glass encountered Sergeant Evans masticating a tough cheese sandwich.

'No. It all ended very satisfactorily. The leader shot himself in the head. Of course, it would have saved a lot of bother if he had done that in the first place. But what about Cheltenham? Did you go in the end? That was a bad accident.'

'If it was one.'

'What?'

'Nothing. Yes I saw it all.'

'They are flying his parents over from Arizona today.'

'I saw your guvnor too,' said Glass, changing the subject. 'In the Stratford Moat House of all places.'

'What was he doing there?'

'Meeting this bloke Marchant. He told me to pass the message on.'

Evans looked worried. 'I hope Marchant didn't see him talking to you.'

'Not a chance. He was nowhere around.'

'Only you're as inconspicuous as a midget in the Harlem Globetrotters.' Evans's length of service and advancing years (he was turned forty) permitted him to feel justified in speaking thus to his superior.

Glass sprinkled more pepper on to his lukewarm individual steak and kidney pie. 'I never told you about the Willie Leigh 'accident' did I?' he said, switching tack again, and he proceeded to recount to the startled Sergeant the events of the Hennessy and the King George.

Evans paused in the middle of hacking through a frozen chocolate éclair, the regular consumption of which accounted for his considerable girth. 'But if this Gold Cup accident is part of this, surely that makes it manslaughter?'

'Precisely.'

'On the other hand, there must have been dozens of falls since the Hennessy. They cannot all have sinister meanings. Why this one?'

'Just a feeling, Jim.' Glass pushed the uneaten third of his pie away and rose clumsily to his feet. 'Best to look on the bright side. At least I didn't back the bugger.'

He reached his office in time to answer the telephone.

'Is that Detective Chief Inspector Glass?'

'Yes.'

'Jeffrey Leek-Turner here. I wonder if you could call and see me at the Jockey Club sometime today.'

And Glass immediately knew his forebodings were correct.

'It could mean nothing, I suppose,' said Jeffrey Leek-Turner, running a hand through his silver hair. 'But after the other incidents. . . .'

'Quite,' said Glass. It had taken the policeman less than half an hour to reach the offices of the Jockey Club, not far from Robin Knox's old flat in Portman Square.

'Of course, the LSD itself didn't kill him and there is no telling what effect such a dose would have, there are so many other factors to be taken into consideration.'

'But he was known never to take drugs?'

'Not even Aspirin. He was very anti-drug. Your clean cut, All-American boy.'

'Easy enough to slip him a couple of drops on a sugar lump, I suppose.'

'That's as may be, Chief Inspector, but I'm afraid there could be a big scandal blowing up here which could be very damaging to racing. Needless to say, none of this has yet been connected with other events; not that there necessarily is a connection.'

'I don't think you believe that, sir. The point is, we are back to the question we asked before. Why? Why would anyone want to stop Thom Snaipe's horse from winning? If indeed that was the intention behind it and I think we can forget personal vendettas with a different trainer, owner and jockey involved.'

'But the horse never had much of a chance of winning anyway. Not enough to go to those lengths to stop it.'

'But to be certain.'

Leek-Turner spread out his hands on the mahogany desk. 'Anybody in the race, I suppose. But that's ridiculous. Where does one start?'

'With the trainer and owner of Reverend Shaker,' said Glass, briskly. And he made a mental note to ring Nicola Beaton who might have a few ideas. 'If you could help me with the addresses I'll collect my sergeant and we'll commence the investigation forthwith. Er, what happened to that chap you called in?'

'My committee felt that, being of such importance, this matter was better dealt with by Scotland Yard and I must say I agree with them.'

Glass walked back to the Yard. The early spring weather continued and shoppers in Oxford

Street wore short-sleeved dresses in the hope of catching an early tan. Instead of going down Park Lane, he crossed under the subway at Marble Arch and walked through Hyde Park. A string of horses passed in front of Knightsbridge Barracks as he came to the end of the Serpentine and his mind, which had been contemplating a possible coach trip to Southend with Mrs. Lewthwaite, was brought sharply back to the case. He quickened his step.

Within five minutes of his return he summoned Sergeant Moon to his office.

'We're off to the Cotswolds for a couple of days,' he announced. 'At least the fine weather is holding.'

'It'll be almost like a holiday,' beamed Sergeant Moon but Glass was inclined more to pessimism.

'That's about all it will be.'

'You're not expecting results then?'

'What do you think? Who will have anything to tell us?'

'The owner maybe.'

'Lives 5,000 miles away. Next?'

'Er, the trainer perhaps. He's English.'

'Don Bellis? Yes, but he's no connection with the last mishaps. Haile has ridden for him occasionally and Willie a long time ago but nothing this year.'

Moon looked glum. 'Not much hope then?'

'Oh, there is always hope, lad. Never give up. But I always find that information comes to us rather than the other way round. Still, we have to put up a show. By the time we have finished we will probably have interviewed the jockey, trainer and owner of every horse that has fallen this season.'

'Oh dear.'

'Now the big decision,' said Glass, treading firmly on the stub of his seventh Craven A of the morning, 'is do we go now or hang on for a canteen lunch.' He consulted his ex-Navy chronograph. 'Twelve o'clock. We'd never make it in time. Gene Morris is staying at the Queen's Hotel in Cheltenham. Phone them and book us in for a room and dinner, we might as well live well while we can.'

Detective Chief Inspector Knox was lucky to be living at all.

The room was pitch black. Was it still night or were there no windows? He had a searing pain in the back of his head and waves of nausea rose from his stomach as bile in his throat but not high enough to make him vomit.

He collected his thoughts. He remembered walking with Marchant and the two men to Marchant's van and stooping to get in. Then . . . a blank.

Something was wrong with his arms. They seemed to be pinioned behind his back yet separated from his body. A plank, maybe, inserted under his arms and nailed to the wall. His wrists were bound tightly, not together but to the plank.

His legs were similarly separated and bound to opposite sides of another plank. He could not move them an inch.

As his senses returned he wondered about the terrible ache in his shoulders. Then he realised that his feet were not touching the ground. His body was resting solely on the top plank which dug cruelly into his armpits.

Detective Chief Inspector Robin Knox was being CRUCIFIED.

Chapter 18

Gene Morris, racehorse owner, rancher, dollar millionaire and popular figure on the American racing circuit, was with the parents of the dead jockey when the two policemen called to interview him at the Queen's Hotel in Cheltenham. Glass came straight to the point.

'This is the third similar occasion this season when an attempt has been made to stop a horse from winning. There may have been others.'

'I thought racing was well controlled in your country,' said Morris, a big man in a shiny mohair suit. 'No organised crime rings like we get in the States.'

'We had been working on a theory of personal vendettas but I can see no grudge motive in this case. Both yourself and the boy are American and the trainer was not involved in the earlier incidents.'

'So you're back to the crime angle?'

'Yes,' said Glass who didn't like to admit they were back, in reality, to a stone wall.

'So you do not think our son was killed deliberately?' said Mr.Snaipe.

His wife, an attractive woman in her early forties held on to his arm and looked away. Her eyes were swollen from crying.

'No, Mr.Snaipe. Neither do we think that he took drugs. It seems likely that somebody wanted to stop that horse winning and the easiest way to do it was to sabotage the jockey.'

'Not a very foolproof method,' said Mr.Snaipe. 'Much easier to dope the horse.' He wished his son had chosen to stay in the family laundry business.

'But doping the horse is more detectable. Had your son merely fallen off when the drug took effect, there would be no reason to test his blood and the crime would have gone undetected.'

'So there could have been lots of these crimes that you know nothing about, where jockeys have just fallen off?'

Glass admitted sadly that this was indeed the case. 'Which suggests it's not the work of professional criminals. They would not leave so much to chance.'

Gene Morris did not appear satisfied. 'You said that a grudge motive was unlikely because the jockey and myself are American. What the hell difference does that make?'

'I only meant that, as you spend so little time in this country, you have not had time to make enemies.'

'Thom Snaipe had been here for two years. Maybe somebody didn't like him.' This last observation brought streams of fresh tears from the dead jockey's mother and sweat to Glass's brow. He became unsettled when people he was supposed to be interviewing challenged his assumptions. He took out a soiled linen handkerchief inscribed with the inital W, rubbed his forehead, then passed it along to Mrs. Snaipe who was by now sobbing copiously.

'We have found no evidence of this,' said Glass.

'That's not surprising since you'll only have been looking since this morning.' Morris stood up. 'My address in Louisiana is on this card.' He threw down a luminous green object. 'I'm leaving on the seven-thirty flight. Ring me if you have any information.'

'And you, Mr. and Mrs. Snaipe, will you be leaving shortly?'

'No, we're staying on until after the weekend. We have to make the arrangements to fly Thom's body back with us.'

'If there is any news, I'll get in touch with you immediately.' He nodded to Sergeant Moon and led the way back to reception.

'I'm afraid I have bad news,' said the sergeant. 'The hotel's full.'

'What!'

'The booking for dinner still stands but the girl made an error. They don't have one room to spare.'

Glass groaned and took out a Craven A. 'Never mind. I know a little bed and breakfast place in Stratford. We can go there, it's also not far from Don Bellis's stables which is handy.'

'But they might be full.' Moon had visions of being taken to a hostel for down and outs.

'Not for me they won't. I know the landlady rather well,' he explained and didn't go into it any further. He had known Lily Marston in the days before the Compton Road Welfare and Social Club and Mrs. Lewthwaite.

Don Bellis's training establishment lay five miles outside Warwick.

'Big place,' commented Sergeant Moon as they drove into the yard.

'Not as big as Bertie Beaton's. A fair size though.' He stopped the car and they walked alongside the stables towards an office at the end of the yard. Most of the stables were empty, the horses out for their evening exercise, but a large bay nuzzled Glass's arm as he walked close to its stall. He stopped to stroke its head.

'You can't beat the smell of horses,' he said, wrinkling his nose appreciatively.

'Oh yes,' agreed Moon. 'The true smell of the country. Reminds you of green fields and winding streams doesn't it?'

Glass looked at him strangely. 'It reminds me of the Tote.'

A girl came out of one of the stalls. She had long flaxen hair and was carrying a bucket. 'Mr.Bellis in the office?' enquired Glass and she nodded.

Don Bellis sat behind a worn leather-topped light oak desk strewn with papers. It reminded Glass of his own office. Obviously the trainer shared his dislike of paperwork.

'All red tape nowadays,' he commented and held out his identity card.

'I've been expecting you, Chief Inspector.' Don Bellis spoke with a quiet West Country burr. 'Do take a seat.' He pointed to two wooden backed chairs.

'Not had much sleep, sir?' enquired Glass, observing the pasty cheeks and the dark pouches underscoring the trainer's eyes.

'Not much,' admitted Bellis wearily, 'A terrible business this.'

'Quite. Tell me, what was Thom Snaipe like? Did he have any enemies?'

'Good Lord no. He was very quiet and polite; quite a gentleman. Are you saying that this was deliberate?'

'Come now, Mr.Bellis,' said Glass in what he hoped was a menacing voice. 'You know there have already been inquiries regarding other incidents at racecourses this season. And you did say you were expecting us.' He looked the man straight in the eye. 'Thom Snaipe was drugged which is why he fell off his horse and died. Which in my book is murder.'

In the law's book it was more likely to be accidental death but Glass was not concerned with the law. 'Somebody's conscience must be troubling them badly today. How about yourself, Mr.Bellis?' The trainer looked startled. 'Have you any enemies? Somebody you or your family may have upset at some time or other?'

'I have no family, Inspector. My wife passed away some years ago and Belinda, my only daughter, went away.' He blinked. Glass feared Bellis was going to cry and went on hastily.

'Just making sure it wasn't an attempt to get at you, Mr.Bellis.'

'She was only seventeen. He had money. I was only her father.' He took a bottle from his desk drawer and extracted a white tablet which he swallowed. 'Rolaids,' he explained. 'My sister sends them over from Canada. Worry always upsets my stomach.'

'There will be more worry yet, I'm afraid. I shall want a list of all of your horses which have fallen in a race this season. As soon as you can. We want to nip this thing . . .' he was going to say 'in the bud' but already it seemed to have reached flowering proportions.

'Bit stern with him weren't you?' ventured Sergeant Moon as they drove away.

'Was I? Law of the jungle I suppose. He was on the defensive from the start so I naturally assumed the aggressive role.' Not for nothing had he read The Naked Ape. 'Anthropology you know.'

150

'Just the opposite of Gene Morris,' pointed out Moon who never knew when to keep silent. 'You were the defensive one there.' Glass said nothing but his glare was enough. Moon quickly changed the subject. 'What's the next step?'

'I thought we might call on the Beatons. The daughter might have heard something round and about.'

But for once Nicola Beaton was as much in the dark as Glass. 'That could have happened to Willie,' she shuddered. 'It must be a crank doing all this.'

'No, not a crank,' said Glass. 'Whoever it is has gone to a lot of trouble to set up these 'accidents'. And there may be more.' He turned to Bertie. 'I shall want a list of all your horses that have fallen this season. And any that should have won their race but didn't.'

'Looking for a common denominator again?' asked Nikki. 'I can't see one myself.'

Neither could Glass. All he had to look forward to was a lot more interviews and some paperwork. 'Let's go,' he said to Sergeant Moon. 'It's an hour's drive back to Stratford.' He picked up his battered trilby. 'Who would have thought all this, Bertie, that day we met at Newbury?'

His prediction about the accommodation was right. Lily Marston, a buxom woman in her late forties, was delighted to see him and hugged him against her ample cleavage as they stood on the doorstep. 'And this is Sergeant Moon,' introduced Glass, extricating his coat button from the collar of her dress.

'You're lucky dearie,' said the landlady. 'I've just got one single room vacant.'

'Oh good,' said Moon and did not ask where the Chief Inspector would be sleeping. He didn't know how Glass did it. Hardly a dashing figure with his ill-fitting garments and yellowed fingertips yet here was this woman, who bore no small resemblance to Sophia Loren, virtually offering herself to him. He himself looked forward to a lonely night in his single room.

Not five miles away Detective Chief Inspector Knox was even more lonely.

Chinks of light through a boarded up window heralded the dawn and allowed him to see the nature of his prison. He was in some kind of hut. The walls were wooden and the floor appeared to be concrete and was covered, in patches, by soil. Gardening tools hung on one wall and there was a tap in the far corner.

The pain in his shoulders was severe and he kept moving his neck in different directions to alleviate it but to no avail. He had given up trying to loosen his bonds. It would now be Friday, ironically Friday the 13th.

He judged it to be about seven o'clock when the door opened and a girl came in carrying a torch. She had long dark hair and wore jeans and a black leather jacket, studded across the shoulders.

'So you're awake then?' She shone the beam into Knox's eyes.

'Who are you?'

'Never mind. We know who you are. Or what you are. Pig.' She spat at him and he felt the spittle slide down his cheek.

'Where is Marchant?'

'He'll be down later.'

'Where are we?'

'Enough questions. You won't be here that long anyway.' She laughed. Knox did not need to ask where he would be going.

'My shoulders . . .' he began but the girl had switched the torch off and was walking to the door. He heard a padlock being fastened then all was quiet.

Robin Knox experienced the cold fear of a condemned man who knows he has not long to live.

Shula Sun was due in Leeds at lunchtime and there was some confusion at the Midland Hotel when it was realised that 'Jeremy Rowlands' was not to be found, indeed had not slept in his bed.

'Hadn't we better phone the police?' suggested Sandy Heneghan anxiously but Lucerelli did not favour this course of action.

'He's probably got himself a piece of ass. He'll show up.'

'But we have to leave for Leeds in ten minutes.'

'So what? You can take us there in your car.'

Heneghan capitulated. 'I'll leave a message with Reception for Jes to follow us,' he said and murmured unkind thoughts to himself about independent promotion men.

The interviews and visits were highly successful, mainly due to Shula's record being top of the charts. Club and dance hall managers were delighted to have a major star, however temporary, at their venues completely free of charge. Four local radio stations arranged interviews, which meant that there was little time available for them to worry about the non-appearance of their erstwhile guide.

In fact, on the Saturday morning as they stood in the waiting lounge at Heathrow Airport for Shula's flight back to the States, all the importance it merited was a brief comment from Lucerelli to the effect that Jes must 'sure have got his rocks off good on Thursday.'

By which time, Detective Chief Inspector Knox had spent two nights and one day without food and water, hanging from the wall of a summer house in Richard Marchant's garden.

Detective Sergeant Evans was the first to be worried when no word from Knox had reached him by Saturday afternoon. He telephoned Sue who said she thought he was probably at the Yard. And when Evans told her he was not, she became worried too.

The office of Trolfid Records was closed for the weekend. Evans rang Superintendent Page of the Drugs Squad only to be told that his friend from the record company, president James Vaughan, was in Australia on a business trip and was not expected back until the following weekend.

Evans then tried to get in touch with Detective Chief Inspector Glass, the last person to have seen Knox, but he was somewhere in the West Country on a case concerning a dead jockey, said a secretary. Would Sergeant Evans like to leave a message? 'Just tell him to ring me at home,' said Evans.

He rang the Drugs Squad again and spoke to an Inspector Jenkins. 'Richard Marchant?' said the inspector to his query. 'Yes, we know of him. What exactly do you want him for?'

'I just want his address,' said Evans. 'It's very important.'

'Give me five minutes. I'll ring you back.'

The return call took half an hour and was not worth the wait. 'Sorry. We had an address for him in Gloucester but apparently he's no longer there.'

Evans replaced the receiver. Dead end. There was nothing he could do but wait.

It was Saturday lunchtime when Richard Marchant finally confronted Detective Chief Inspector Knox. The policeman was barely conscious but a can of cold water thrown over him brought him to life.

'I'm wasting no time on you,' he announced brusquely. 'We know you're working for the police so we can't afford to let you go. A decision is being made about your disposal. In the meantime you'll stay here.'

'What about food and water?' gasped Knox. 'If the orders are to keep me alive, they'll not thank you for starving me to death.'

Marchant was at the door before he had finished speaking. 'I have nothing more to say.' Light from the garden flooded in as he opened the door. 'Nobody will find you here, dead or alive.'

And, as he spoke, Detective Chief Inspector Glass was questioning racehorse trainers not two miles away at Stratford on Avon racecourse.

Chapter 19

Susan Knox spent a sleepless night and on Sunday morning had still not heard from her husband. Her father turned up at lunchtime and was disturbed at his son-in-law's disappearance.

'And you say Jim Evans hasn't seen or heard from him since I met him in the Moat House at Stratford?'

'That's right. Do you think something has happened to him?'

'Not necessarily, Sue. This is undercover work.' But his reply was unconvincing. He rang Sergeant Evans at home. 'Any news, Jim?'

'Not a thing and the wife has been in all the time to take messages.' He searched for something to say. 'How is the racing job going?'

'A complete blank,' admitted Glass. 'No motive, no witnesses, no evidence. Just like before, really. No reason to believe anything is wrong.'

'Until the next time.'

'Precisely. All the owners and trainers are terrified of letting their horses near a racecourse.'

'Can you blame them?' There was a silence; both men afraid to voice their fears about the missing detective. Then, 'I'll phone you if I hear anything,' said Evans at last.

'Have you tried all the people from the record company?'

'The singer and her manager have gone back to America, their photo was in today's Sunday Megaphone, and the record company is shut till tomorrow.'

'And he was definitely due back yesterday?'

'As soon as their plane left.'

'We'll just have to wait I suppose. All we seem to do in both these cases is wait. And usually something awful happens.'

He did not have to wait much longer.

The girl in the black leather jacket and jeans sat in the lounge of Richard Marchant's house, looking through the French windows down the long garden, which led to the banks of the river. She was smoking a joint, sucking the smoke deeply into her lungs, and listening to a Whitesnake album on the expensive Sony stereo system.

The mild spring had brought out the flowers and a dazzling display of daffodils surrounded the old summerhouse where Detective Chief Inspector Knox was nailed to the wall.

The imprisonment was beginning to worry her. Marchant had issued strict orders that she was not to go near the summerhouse but she was concerned. It was dangerous keeping him there so long. Granted he was unlikely to escape but the police would be searching for him. She took a phial of powder from her handbag and sniffed the white substance therefrom up her nostrils.

Lynne had not always been a drug addict.

As a child she had attended a strict convent school where nuns ruled with an iron rod and rumours abounded of novices having to kneel on dried peas as a penance for minor misdemeanours, a fiction lifted from 'The Awful Disclosures of Maria Monk' which circulated amongst the girls.

The outside world intruded little, leaving the girls innocent and untouched, so that when they were let out at the tender age of eighteen, they were easy prey for seasoned seducers.

Lynne was still a few weeks short of her eighteenth birthday when she met hers. He was good looking, sophisticated and rich. He took her to exciting places, bought her drinks with strange names and treated her like a lady.

The fact that he was old enough to be her father, was notorious for his affairs with young girls and was still technically married to his last wife did nothing to deter her.

He introduced her to people she recognised from the television screen. Then he introduced her to cannabis. All the smart people used it, he told her, and she believed him. She believed him when he told her they used cocaine as well. She sniffed it, rubbed it in her gums and licked it with her tongue. At first she did not care for it but he encouraged her to persevere and she started to take it regularly.

Until she could not do without it.

One day his divorce came through. She had always hoped he would want to marry again quickly and he did. The first she knew of it was an announcement in the Daily Telegraph and his bride was described as an attractive heiress of twenty-one.

Which left her, at eighteen, alone, broken-hearted and . . . a drug addict.

She had seen Richard Marchant at some of the parties she had been to. He was on the fringe of the rock scene, the social equivalent in the seventies of Hollywood in the thirties. Marchant had many friends and he knew how to turn such relationships to his advantage.

She never knew how he got her number but a few days after her estrangement he rang her at home and invited her to a party. She was not particularly keen but she was running low on cocaine and there would be a good chance of getting some if she went.

It came as a surprise when she learned Marchant himself was the main supplier.

'I'm afraid I haven't much money,' she said.

'I don't want money,' he smiled but he was not a man who did favours for nothing. The deal he offered was that she should help him 'merchandise' his drugs in return for a regular supply. It would be her job to encourage the smaller customers to increase their consumption and get new ones hooked.

If necessary by using her body.

She agreed and within a month had left her home and family to live with him in his Streatham bedsit. Within eighteen months, they had graduated to the house in Stratford. She never knew where Marchant obtained his supplies but a man called Taylor rang from time to time. . . .

The telephone rang. 'I've seen Taylor,' said Richard Marchant, 'and we are to get rid of the pig tonight. Fetch the Mercedes from the garage. It might be risky using the Transit.'

'Where are you taking him?'

'Don't ask questions. Leave me to worry about that. Just pick up the car like I tell you.' He rang off.

She did not know why she went to the summerhouse. Knox blinked in the sudden light as she threw open the door. His lips were cracked, his mouth parched, his cheeks sunken. The pain from his shoulder had become part of his whole existence and he hovered between lucidity and delirium. He saw the girl and tried to talk but he was able only to mouth the one word. 'H-e-l-p.'

And somewhere, deep inside her soul, Lynne felt a compelling stirring of compassion. She could not let this man die. She ran back to the house to find a knife to cut him free but then she stopped. Richard would know it was she who had released him. Then he might kill her instead. She had no illusions about his protestations of love.

There must be another way. And then it came to her. She would phone the police anonymously and tell them where the prisoner was. Wait a minute. Richard might return and not see the police car up the drive until it was too late. She would have to wait down the road and head him off. She would tell him she had seen the police arrive and escaped through the back gardens.

She picked up the telephone and dialled 999.

'Emergency. Which service do you require?'

'Police.'

'What number are you speaking from?'

She had not bargained for this. She hesitated. She could not give her own number.

'What number are you speaking from, caller?'

'Er, Stratford 5831.' It was the hospital number. She hoped thay would not recognise it.

'Police emergency.'

She was through. 'Hello, police?' She realised that she was trembling. 'Can you come quickly? There's a man in the summer house and I think he's dead.' She gave the address and before they could ask questions she hung up. There was no time to lose. She ran out of the house to the corner of the road and slowed to walking pace as she turned towards the town centre and the garage. The police car passed her, siren blaring, when she was a safe quarter of a mile away.

At the garage she collected the Mercedes, which had been in for a service, and drove to the

A46 to watch out for Richard. Now that she had done it she was frightened of the repercussions. There was going to be big trouble ahead.

'Bloody hell, out here Bob, quickly.' P.C. Nigel Mulcaster gazed in horror at the semi-conscious figure of Detective Chief Inspector Knox hanging from the wall of the summerhouse.

'Better radio for an ambulance,' he said, taking the two-way radio from beneath his tunic. 'I wonder who the poor devil is.' He regarded Knox's jeans and sweat shirt. 'Looks like a biker to me.'

'Bit old for that,' said Bob. 'He certainly upset someone.' He hunted around the floor for some sort of tool to help prise the planks from the wall and found an old chisel. 'This is going to be a CID job I reckon. Better call the station and have them send someone down to search the house.'

It was going to be more than just a CID job.

When it was discovered who the prisoner really was, an immediate telephone call was made to London and Scotland Yard took over the case.

Richard Marchant's girl friend intercepted him on the road to Stratford and broke the news about the arrival of the police.

'I got out through the back,' she explained uneasily.

'Who the hell could have told the pigs he was there? That's what I want to know.'

'Perhaps someone was tailing him.'

'Since Thursday? Don't be stupid.'

'Well perhaps they followed you from the club, lost you, then saw the van later on by accident and followed it to the house.' She spoke desperately, terrified that Marchant would realise that it was all her doing.

'One thing is certain,' he said. 'We can't go back there and we're going to have to hide somewhere. They'll be looking for us.'

'We can leave the Transit here and go in the Merc.' They were in a lay-by on the A46. 'They won't know that.'

'If there are road blocks up we'll be stopped whatever we're driving. We'd be better on the bus. Separately. We'll leave both cars here and travel on different buses. I'll meet you in Birmingham tonight and meanwhile I'll ring Taylor and see what he has to say.'

'I'm frightened Richard. What if they catch us?'

'We'll probably be tried for attempted murder,' said Richard Marchant calmly. 'I'll be in the back row of the Tivoli Cinema in Station Street at seven o'clock. Remember, from now on we're on the run.'

The Monday morning edition of The Megaphone featured the story prominently on its front page. A photograph of the summer house accompanied the banner headline 'CRUCIFIED' and mention was made in the text that the police were anxious to interview Richard Marchant whom they believed might be able to help them with their enquiries. It was thought he could be travelling with a girl friend. Identikit drawings of the couple appeared on Page Two.

'Not a bad likeness,' approved Richard Marchant. 'The expression is wrong, of course, but he hasn't got bad observation, considering.'

'What you mean is we are stuck in this flea pit because everybody in the streets will recognise us?' Lynne was sprawled on the bed in bra and jeans.

The fugitive couple had spent the night in a seedy hotel near Birmingham's New Street Station. The owner was a friend of Marchant's who could be relied on to keep quiet.

'I rang Taylor. He says to lie low for a few days and get in touch with him again at the end of the week.'

'Not six more days in this hole?' The sheets were off-white, the mattress dipped in the middle and between them they had only the clothes they were wearing when they left Stratford. Marchant, who had worn the same pair of jeans for the last six months, was not too concerned about this but Lynne was not happy. 'What about clean clothes and food?'

'Arthur will bring us food in. What do you want clothes for? You're not going anywhere.'

'Why can't we skip the country? We could get forged passports. We could be in Amsterdam by tomorrow.' Her voice had an hysterical edge but Marchant knew how to deal with that. He took some cocaine from his wallet.

'Here you are, have some of this. I knew we should have killed that pig in the first place.'

Lynne sniffed the drug up her nostrils. All this was her fault. By saving the policeman she had put their whole future in jeopardy. 'Yes,' she said. 'Then why didn't you?'

'If I see him again,' said Richard Marchant, 'you can be sure I will.'

Superintendent Cecil Page of the Drugs Squad was the third person to visit Detective Chief Inspector Knox in Stratford on Avon's General Hospital, being preceded by the patient's wife and Sergeant Evans.

'Very unfortunate business, this,' he commented bitterly. 'They seem to have escaped our net completely.'

Knox, who thought it was unfortunate for different reasons, lay back in his bed and said nothing. His shoulders still ached and he was feeling frail. He was under observation.

'And you got no leads at all?' persisted the superintendent unsolicitously. Knox shook his head and caught the eye of the ward sister who immediately came over.

'I'm sorry but I must ask you to leave now. The patient needs complete rest,' and she escorted the protesting officer away, turning only to give a broad wink to the relieved detective.

His next visitor was more welcome. 'So much for the patients' mid-day rest,' he said, struggling to a sitting position. 'We could hear you clattering in from the other side of the hospital.'

Detective Chief Inspector Glass grinned. 'It's these regulation boots. Weigh a ton they do. How are you feeling?'

'Not so bad now. Would you like a grape?'

'No thanks. I've just had my dinner.' He eyed the clumps of black grapes topping a bowl of miscellaneous fruit. 'Keeping your bowels working I see.'

'There are two more bowls beside those. Sergeant Evans's wife must have her own orchard.'

'He's been up then has he?'

'Yesterday.'

'Caused quite a stir at the Yard I hear, when the news came in.'

'I can imagine,' said Knox drily.

'Bit of a cock-up this case. You get no further than Marchant and the Drugs Squad knew about him anyway.'

'And who do we blame for that? If you hadn't come barging up at the Moat House?'

'Now then, don't get your back up, if you'll pardon the expression. How is the shoulder by the way?'

'Very sore thank you. Is there any news on Marchant yet?'

'I don't know. I have been in Newmarket all week on this racing job.'

'Still nothing doing on that?'

'Not a thing.' Glass made another inspection of the fruit bowl and selected a banana. 'Looks like Marchant got away then.'

'Disappeared off the face of the earth so Evans said. The Drugs Squad turned the house upside down but no sign of him or the girl.'

'Oh yes, the girl. I never saw her.'

'We think she dialled the 999 call. She came into the shed a few minutes before the local lads turned up.'

'Reckon she got cold feet?'

'I suppose so. No other reason. Marchant won't be so pleased with her if he finds out.'

'If. I presume she'll be with him?'

'Don't know.' He rearranged the pillows behind his back to alleviate the strain of sitting upright. 'There were no leads in the house. Did you know that that place is owned by a bottling company? They use it to accommodate members of their staff.'

'So Marchant works for a bottling company?'

'No he doesn't; at least there is no mention of him on the payroll for the last five years which is when the house was purchased. No, Evans did some checking and it turns out it was occupied by a former sales manager who left twelve months ago. Apparently nobody in the company wanted to take it on so they rented it out.'

'To Marchant?'

'It was let through an estate agent, all in the open. Marchant applied, he had the cash, so they let it to him on a two year lease. There is one strange thing though.'

'Yes?'

'The managing director of the bottling company is your friend Lord Crossens.'

'Really?' Glass swallowed the last of his banana and searched for a suitable receptacle in which to deposit the skin.

'Odd coincidence isn't it? But I suppose a bottling company is an obvious acquisition for a jam manufacturer.'

Glass said nothing. But he did not believe in coincidences.

The next day Music Week, the reord industry 'Bible', was published showing Shula Sun's record still at No.1 in the charts.

Meanwhile, the singer was back in the States promoting her new single over there whilst Lucerelli prepared to fly out to Norway on tour with a heavy metal band called Transport.

Detective Chief Inspector Glass spent the rest of the week interviewing jockeys and trainers with Sergeant Moon but was unable to find evidence of any other races where foul play might have been suspected.

In the meantime, Detective Chief Inspector Knox was released from hospital in Stratford on Avon and, on the Friday, attended a meeting at Scotland Yard with Superintendent Page of the Drugs Squad.

'There has been no word of Marchant or the girl. My men have questioned all their known associates and nobody has seen them.'

'You think they're still in the country?' asked Knox.

'I think so, yes.'

'Then I know one way we might ferret them out.'

'What's that?'

'We put a piece in the newspapers 'revealing' that Marchant himself rang the police to release me. We say we are afraid he may be in danger and offer him some sort of amnesty if he gives himself up.'

Page pondered. 'It could work. But won't he say it was the girl and not him?'

'Maybe, but will they believe him? Whoever it is giving Marchant his orders, he'll not risk mistakes. These men are professionals. And killers.'

'If this article works, they'll be after Marchant.'

'Who might prefer to take his chance with us.'

'If he ever gets to us. You could be signing his death warrant.'

Knox thought back to his three days hanging from the wall of the summer house. 'Yes,' was all he said.

Richard Marchant and Lynne were still in bed at ten o'clock on Monday morning when the landlord of the hotel pushed the paper under the door.

The seven days that had elapsed since Knox was found had relegated the kidnapping to a brief paragraph in the middle pages. Therefore, the shock to Marchant to find his face once more on the front page was considerable.

POLICE   NAME   INFORMER   ran the headline.

In a statement issued today, Scotland Yard revealed that a 27 year old rock musician, Richard Marchant, who is wanted in connection with the recent abduction of Detective Chief Inspector Robin Knox, may be in some danger of his life. It is believed that it was Marchant who alerted police to the detective's whereabouts when he was given orders to kill him. Consequently, other members of the gang could be afraid he will turn 'supergrass' and so put out a contract to have him silenced.

Detective Chief Inspector Knox, at the time of the kidnapping, was involved in an undercover operation investigating a national drugs organisation.

'Christ,' said Marchant when he read it. 'That's done it.'

Lynne took The Megaphone from him and read the front page. 'What will happen?' she said, not daring to tell him how near the truth the article was.

'If Taylor believes that then I'm a dead man,' said Marchant simply. He was under no illusions about the man he worked for. 'I must ring him immediately.'

'Use the payphone downstairs. You musn't risk going out.'

He stopped in the act of putting on his jeans. 'It says here,' he said, picking up the paper again, 'that somebody alerted the police.'

'So?' said Lynne nervously.

'Just that we were not followed in the van. And the only people that knew where we had taken that pig were Rodney, Lionel and . . . you.'

'What are you saying?'

'It was you wasn't it? Rodney and Lionel wouldn't say anything.'

'Richard.' She was sobbing now. 'He was going to die.' She clutched at his arm but he hit her across the mouth and she rolled back on the bed.

'You stupid bitch. Too right he was going to die. You stupid cow.' He stormed out of the room and telephoned his superior.

'Don't do anything for the time being,' ordered Taylor. 'You say the girl is still with you?'

'Yes,' said Marchant. 'How was I to know she would do something stupid like that?'

'Don't worry about it. Just lie low and give me a ring tomorrow. We will organise something for you and we will take care of the girl. Do nothing for the present.'

Taylor hung up and sat for a moment thinking, then he picked up the phone again and dialled a number.

'It's Taylor, sir,' he said and recounted the conversation with Marchant. 'I take it you've read the piece in The Megaphone?'

'Yes,' was the reply. 'We cannot afford any leaks, Taylor. They must both be eliminated. I'll leave that up to you.'

'Very good, sir,' Taylor replaced the receiver. From that moment Richard Marchant was a dead man.

Chapter 21

The young coloured man in red singlet and white silk trunks was on his thirty-ninth press-up when the phone rang in his St.John's Wood flat.

Erskine Porter had not been born to such luxury. He originated from a terraced slum in Hackney, the product of an unlikely union between a black Portuguese seaman and a part Cherokee chambermaid from the Savoy Hotel. He was brought up by foster parents, a quiet introverted child who had little to do with other children except when they taunted him about his walnut colouring. Whereupon he beat them up, savagely. Word soon got around about his pugilistic dexterity and thenceforth he was left alone.

He quit school at sixteen, resigned to the fact that a half-caste youth with no qualifications was unlikely to find a job in England with unemployment running higher than at any time since the Thirties. Therefore he decided to use his best asset to earn himself a living. His body.

Every day he trained at the local gym, working to a strict routine of weightlifting, bodybuilding and exercises. At nights, he worked as a bouncer in local night clubs to supplement his dole. At nineteen, he was 6ft. 2ins. tall and weighed twelve stones, all solid muscle. He graduated from bouncer to bodyguard or, in the parlance of the East End, 'minder'.

One day, whilst looking after a visiting Arab, he had occasion to defend his charge against an armed attacker. Calmly, Porter stabbed his assailant through the heart and, to his surprise, found the experience exhilarating. And, at that moment, he discovered his life's vocation. He would be a hit man. Word soon got round that his services were available. He charged high prices which he was able to justify by his efficiency and discretion. Porter's victims died quietly, to order and with no trace of thekiller.

And quite often with no trace of the victim either.

By the time he moved into the St.John's Wood flat he was charging £10,000 a contract. There were men willing to pay this price for the removal of a fellow human being.

Erskine Porter let the telephone ring until he had completed his fiftieth press-up, then jumped effortlessly to his feet to answer it.

'Hello,' said a voice. 'I want to speak to Mr.Porter. My name is Taylor.'

Richard Marchant and Lynne passed the day in uneasy silence in the claustrophobic hotel room. He told her nothing of the conversation he had had with Taylor, that she was to be 'dealt with'. He imagined that, once she was out of the way, Taylor would arrange for him to be sent abroad until the heat had died down, maybe to Amsterdam where the drug trade was flourishing. He felt no remorse for what might happen to the girl.

At six o'clock he went to phone Taylor again.

'Is the girl still with you?'

'Yes.'

'And she doesn't suspect anything is going to happen to her?'

'Nothing more than a severe reprimand.'

'Good. I want you to go to a village called Temple Grafton, outside Stratford, take the girl with you.'

'How will we get there?'

'You will find a Ford Escort parked outside the hotel at eight o'clock. The ignition keys will be in it.'

'And when we reach Temple Grafton?'

'There is a telephone kiosk in the middle of the village. Park in the side road and ring me from there. But, this is important, leave the girl in the car.'

'What is going to happen to her?'

'Never mind that, it's not your worry. Now have you got all that?'

Marchant repeated his instructions. 'What about when it's all over?'

'I'll speak to you about that when you phone me from Temple Grafton. I shall expect to hear from you at 8.45.p.m. And don't let the girl suspect anything is wrong.'

'Do me a favour,' said Richard Marchant scornfully. 'Do you take me for a fool?'

He could not see the smile on the other's face as he replaced the receiver.

The Ford Escort was dark blue and waiting outside the hotel as promised.

Lynne was apprehensive about the trip. 'What do we have to go to this Temple Grafton place for?'

'To change cars,' lied Marchant. 'Taylor is going to help us out of the country.'

'What did he say about me telling the police?'

'He was a bit annoyed at first but I managed to calm him down.' He put his arm round her shoulders as a gesture of affection although he would have held her head on the guillotine block just as readily.

They drove along the country lanes off the Alcester Road, the dark roads unlit by street light or moon.

'I hope he'll provide us with a change of clothes. I'm stinking in this T-shirt and jeans.'

'You won't have to wear them much longer,' said Marchant truthfully.

'We're coming up to the village now.' He drove around for a minute till he saw the phone box. The village was deserted. He saw a little side road and reversed into it, parking the Escort under cover of some large sycamore trees. 'You wait in the car,' he said.

'Can't I come with you? I don't like it here.'

'No. I'm only going to make a phone call. I shan't be a minute.' He jumped out of the car and walked slowly across the road to the kiosk. He wondered, as he walked on, what method they would use to kill her. A shot might startle the inhabitants of the village. Maybe strangulation? Or a blow to the head with a crowbar? Not much room for that in the front seat of an Escort. He pulled open the red phone booth door, picked up the receiver and dialled Taylor's number. He listened, first to the clicks then the ringing tone followed by the pips. He started to push his ten pence into the slot and so intent was he on his task that he never noticed the black figure steal noiselessly beside him until the sharp silver blade sliced into his throat, severing the carotid artery and cutting off the main supply of blood to his brain.

'Good evening Mr.Taylor,' said Erskine Porter, pleasantly, taking the telephone from the late

Richard Marchant's hands. 'Half the job is completed. I shall be in touch.'

He stepped carefully round the slumped figure, avoiding the spurts of fresh red blood gushing from the open wound. Nobody was about. Now for the girl. He walked quickly over to the side road. His intention was to kill her as she sat in the car then drive to the phone box, load Marchant's body into the boot and dispose of the two corpses before dawn.

His expectations were quickly dashed.

When Erskine Porter reached the side road, the Ford Escort had disappeared.

Lynne sat in the front passenger seat of the Escort and watched Richard Marchant walk across to the telephone booth. She was frightened. Why had they come to this out of the way spot just to change cars? Why change cars at all? And where was the other vehicle? Something was wrong. Suddenly she heard a rustle outside the car. Frantically she fumbled for the door lock. Then it was at the other side, a scratching at the driver's door. She scrambled across the seats and pressed the catch down on the offside window. Only then did she see a ginger cat walking away.

Her heart was thumping. She felt she was in mortal danger. Richard had turned the bend and was out of sight. Then she saw the shadow of a man creeping towards the phone kiosk. It was the nature of his walk that attracted her attention, that of a hunter stalking his prey. She could stand it no longer. With shaking hands she turned on the ignition, slipped the gear lever into reverse and quietly edged the car backwards down the lane. A few hundred yards along she rounded a bend and saw she had passed a cart track running at a sharp angle off the road into a field. Quickly, she changed into first gear and let the car run forwards to halt in a clover covered meadow.

Minutes passed. She opened the window so that she would hear the noise of anyone approaching but not a sound disturbed the stillness of the night.

She wondered if she dared walk back and look for Richard. What would he do? Would he be looking for her? What would he do if he found her? Or had something awful happened to him? All she knew was she must stay hidden at least until daylight. Once or twice she thought she heard the hum of distant car engines but nobody came down the lane.

She closed the car window, checked the door locks and settled down to rest. By midnight she was fast asleep.

At one o'clock a grey XJ6 driven by Erskine Porter edged its way down the lane. . .

Chapter 22

Grant Heathcliffe sat on the terrace of the restaurant outside the Royal Shakespeare Theatre drinking a cup of coffee and surveying the River Avon flowing gently below.

Grant, born Harold Crossley, was a member of the Royal Shakespaeare Company, an ambition he had cherished since he first paraded in his mother's dress at his fifth birthday party in Leighton Buzzard.

His penchant for dressing up in ladies' clothing never left him so he was well suited to a career which allowed him this luxury although in the present production he had to content himself with a toga.

He liked Stratford. He enjoyed the professional camaraderie at the Dirty Duck, the pub behind the theatre. The old buildings in the town fascinated him and he was entranced with the surrounding countryside. More than anything he relished the adulation of the fans, being pointed at in the street, receiving invitations to open garden parties, judge baby shows, speak to golf clubs, all of which he accepted.

Both his ill-fated affairs with celebrated actresses had received generous linage in the gutter press. Less so his affair with an unknown actor. He revelled in the publicity taking advantage of any circumstance to be in the spotlight.

As he gazed across the river from the terrace his eye caught a shapeless bundle bumping against the bank. Curiosity prompted him to stand up and peer over the edge. He could not quite believe what he saw so he walked round past the theatre entrance and down to the banks for a closer inspection. He prodded the object with his toe and his suspicions were confirmed.

Excitedly he ran into the theatre foyer to phone, first to a contact on the local paper, secondly to a friend at The Megaphone, to whom he offered the 'exclusive story' and, almost as an afterthought, the police.

This done, he returned quickly to the river bank. Luckily, the object had caught on a promontory on the bank and had not floated away. He gave it another nudge with his foot to verify he had not been mistaken. He had not. How fortuitous, he thought, that the riverbank was deserted on an early March morning. This would be front-page stuff indeed.

And it was. The next day The Megaphone carried a front page picture of the celebrated Shakespearian actor, Grant Heathcliffe, pointing at the river where the sodden remains of Richard Marchant had been dragged from the water.

'Dead less than twenty-four hours and that is the nearest I can say,' the local pathologist informed Detective Chief Inspector Knox who had driven up to Stratford to identify the body. 'The body being in water and all that.'

'How did he die? Drowning?'

'Oh no. Knifed in the throat. Somebody who knew what he was doing I would say. Cut him in just the right place. He would have died in seconds. Messy though.'

'You mean we should be looking for bloodstains?'

'If you knew where to look. The impression I get is that he was killed some time before he entered the water so his body was probably transported from the place he was murdered.'

'Which could be anywhere within fifty miles.'

'Or a hundred if the murderer was a fast driver. There was also this.' He held up a length of chain. The other end was attached to Marchant's ankle. 'They obviously didn't want us to find him. I would say this came adrift from a heavy weight of some description. By rights he should have been at the bottom of the river.'

'Concrete boots, eh?' said Knox, looking at the man who had nailed him to the wall of the summer house. 'Shades of the Mafia.'

'A gang murder is it?'

'Something like that,' replied Knox non-committally. 'Certainly I shall want to search the river.'

'What?'

'It'll be a big job dredging that lot.'

'But whatever for?'

'Because,' said the Scotland Yard man importantly, 'there is also a young girl missing.'

'Good Lord. And you think she may be in the river too?'

'The frogmen will tell us that but, yes, I think it very likely. Except, in her case, the weights attached to her body did not come adrift.' He held the chains in his hands. 'I think we'll find her at the bottom of the Avon.'

In this last assumption, Robin Knox was wrong. Lynne slept peacefully through the night across the front seats of the Ford Escort in the field at Temple Grafton. She woke at seven-thirty, stiff but unharmed.

Erskine Porter in his XJ6 had passed within ten yards of her but she had chosen her hiding place well. The track was only visible to somebody going the opposite way up the lane. Porter had driven right past it and carried on driving out of the village.

Lynne cautiously stepped out of the car onto the dewy grass to stretch her legs. She did not know what to do next. Richard Marchant would be looking for her, thinking she had betrayed him. He might assume she was ready to give herself up to the police in which case he would be anxious to silence her.

Alternatively, remembering the man who had crept towards the phone kiosk, something could have happened to Richard. In which case, the same people would undoubtedly be after her.

Either way she was in danger. She had to get away.

She got back in the Escort and started the engine.

Certainly she did not want to hang around Temple Grafton. She backed carefully into the lane. Already the morning sun was casting a pale glow over the budding hedgerows.

She drove slowly through the village, not sure what she expected to see. She stopped at the phone box. Nothing untoward. She went in and picked up the telephone. Dialling tone as normal. The usual graffiti, carved, sprayed and written, adorned the interior.

She missed the two spots of Richard Marchant's blood on the floor beneath her shoes.

Where could she go? Stratford could be ruled out, the police would still be looking for her there. Birmingham was out too. Taylor might expect her to go back to the hotel, besides which he would recognise her car. So would Richard Marchant.

She did not know that, at that moment, he was floating down the River Avon.

She looked round. The village was deserted still. She decided to drive to Oxford. Dressed as she was she would be reasonably inconspicuous amongst the undergraduates and cheap accommodation would be easy to find, she thought, in a city with a large student population.

The journey took longer than she anticipated because she got caught up in the morning rush hour traffic. In the Escort she could have been mistaken for an ordinary citizen on her way to work but she knew the reality was different. She was on the run.

Her big mistake had been to leave the Stratford house so quickly that she forgot to pick up any money. She had only twelve pounds on her, no change of clothes, no food and . . . no cocaine.

Finding somewhere to stay proved as easy as she had hoped. She got a cheap bed sitting room in a large lodging house near the colleges and paid the owner £10 for the first week's rent. Most of the remaining two pounds went on buying food that she took back to her room to eat.

Her next task was to find a job to earn some money. As she had never worked since leaving college, she had no insurance card or credentials. So the Jobcentre was out. She would have to find casual labour.

The trouble was, she was afraid to go out in case she was recognised. For the same reason she dismissed the idea of shoplifting. The consequences if she got caught were too great.

She stayed in her room all day, the craving for cocaine growing by the hour. As soon as early evening arrived, she went round the pubs offering her services as a barmaid but barmaids were plentiful in Oxford.

She returned, dispirited, to the room and slept badly on the bare mattress.

The next morning she decided to buy the local paper to check through the Situations Vacant columns in the hope there might be some job that required no documents or references.

In the small corner newsagent's, she flicked through the papers on the counter and stopped in horror. Her Identikit photograph was back on the front page of The Megaphone. Next to it was a picture of Grant Heathcliffe beside the River Avon under the headline ACTOR FINDS MURDERED MAN IN SHAKESPEARE'S RIVER. Hurriedly she picked up the paper, handed across 12p and ran all the way home to read the article.

Senior police officials, it informed her, feared she was in mortal danger, if she was not resting on the bottom of the River Avon already, and appealed to her to give herself up.

So she had been right about the man at the phone box. She remembered his walk clearly. He must have killed Richard and he would still be after her. Taylor must have ordered this. She must get away, out of the country if possible. She was too frightened to give herself up to the police. What was it Richard said? Attempted murder?

Who could she turn to? She and Richard had no friends. To Richard friends were business.

She thought of her father. It was two years since she had left home and the parting was bitter.

There had been rows about her association with her older man followed by more rows about Richard and the drugs, culminating in her abrupt departure to move in with Richard. She had seen her father just once since then, accidentally passing him in the street whilst doing some early Christmas shopping in Birmingham.

She had ignored him.

She paced round the small room. It was forty-eight hours since she had had a fix and she was on edge. She told herself she must not panic.

One person might help her, her former lover. She had not seen him since his marriage to the heiress but she felt he owed her a favour. After all, it was he who had introduced her to drugs and then deserted her. He could well afford to give her enough money to get out of the country.

With new determination, she walked down to the phone box at the end of the road. She still knew his number off by heart. Her hand trembled as she put in her five pence in answer to the pips. A cultured voice spoke. 'Good morning. Lord Crossens's residence.'

'Excuse me, sir, there is a young lady on the telephone, says she wishes to speak to you personally and that it is important.'

Lord Crossens sat alone at the breakfast table, resplendent in a scarlet silk dressing-gown, a mug of coffee in one hand and a folded Financial Times in the other. 'At this time? Why can't she phone the office? How did she get this number? Who is she?'

The butler deliberated whilst he endeavoured to assimilate this rapid flow of questions. Eventually he managed only one answer out of the possible four. 'She did not give her name, sir.'

'Well go back and ask her.'

'Yes sir.'

The seventeenth Earl put down the Financial Times, drank the last of the coffee and picked up The Megaphone. He allowed the front page a cursory glance, that poof Grant Heathcliffe had fished somebody out of the river, before turning to the racing columns. William Hill's were offering 6-1 against Sailor's Delight winning the Grand National, half the odds he had got when he placed his own £5,000 bet three months ago. He smiled at the thought. He would win the race without a doubt. He was just two days away from achieving his life's ambition.

The butler returned noiselessly. 'It is a person called Lynne on the phone, sir. She says you will know who she is.' The butler had been in Lord Crossens's service only twelve months and knew nothing of Lady Crossens's precursors, but he could tell by the Earl's startled reaction that the call was unwelcome.

'Put it through to my study, Cowles. I will take it there.' He put down the paper irritably. Why was she ringing him after all this time? He did not like hearing from ex-girl friends, especially this one. The police were after her too which meant more trouble. He had read the papers. He carefully closed the study door before speaking. 'Hello.'

'Neville, it's Lynne.'

'Yes?'

'I'm sorry for ringing but I need your help. I'm in trouble.'

'How can I help?' His tone was not encouraging.

'Can you lend me some money?'

'You mean give, don't you?'

'All right, if you like, give.' She spoke defiantly. 'I want to get out of the country. The police are after me.'

'You have no chance. They'll be watching the ports and airports.'

She had not thought of that. 'What can I do?'

'Where are you now?'

'Oxford. It's serious, Neville. They want me for attempted murder.' She faltered. 'And I need some coke.'

'On the snort too are you?'

'It was you who first made me take it,' she blazed. 'So you can help me.'

'Calm down.' He spoke sharply. 'I'll help you. Can you get to Birmingham?'

'Yes, but I'm afraid of being recognised. Some men might be after me as well. Friends of Richard Marchant. He's a drug. Deale. I was going out with him. Well they've killed him.'

He cut short her breathless gabble.

'I can't see you until this evening. Go to New Street Station, buy a platform ticket and I'll meet you on Platform 6a.'

'You will turn up?'

'Six o'clock.' He replaced the receiver abruptly and sat for a moment in his red leather swivel chair, deep in thought. Then he picked up the phone again and dialled a number.

'Sometimes,' he said, with preamble, 'I do not know what I pay for. Especially when I have to do the jobs myself. Now listen carefully. The girl will be at New Street Station tonight at six o'clock, on Platform 6a. Have you got that? Right.'

'The first train that comes into that platform, I want her UNDERNEATH IT. And this time, Taylor, there must be no mistake.'

Erskine Porter had not returned to London satisfied with his mission in the Midlands. Having received only a down payment for the contract, he was unlikely to see the rest until he had completed the work. The problem was, he had no idea where to locate the girl, indeed, he did not even know her name. The front page of The Megaphone carried her Identikit picture but England was a big place.

Luckily Mr.Taylor was able to assist him.

'I'm not pleased with the way things have gone, Mr.Porter. You've slipped up badly on this assignment.' Even allowing for the poor telephone reception his voice sounded distinctly gruff.

'Not my fault that she drove off.'

'And why do you think she did drive away, in my car incidentally?'

'I don't know.'

'Could it have been because she decided to follow her boyfriend to the kiosk and thus was able to observe the spectacle of you cutting his throat? Because, if so, then she could make a very interesting witness if you were tried for murder.'

Erskine Porter said nothing. It was a possibility he himself had considered.

'However, we have located the girl for you so you'll have the opportunity to complete your task.'

'Where is she?'

'At six o'clock this evening she will be on Platform 6a of New Street Station in Birmingham. I don't want her to leave that station.'

'Are you crazy? In front of all those people?'

'Mr. Porter, I was not suggesting you mow her down with a machine gun in front of horrified homegoing commuters. My idea was more in the nature of an accident. A little gentle nudge as the train comes in, she is crushed to death beneath the wheels and you slip quietly into the crowd, easy enough in Birmingham with your colour.'

'I don't like it.'

'You don't have to like it. Just do it if you want your money. And when it's all over, ring me with the good news. That's all.'

Erskine Porter had no choice. Irrespective of the fee or Taylor's attitude, the girl might have seen him kill Marchant. She had to be silenced. He set off for Birmingham.

Lunch for Lynne was the remains of a bag of peanuts and the last of three sausage rolls she had bought the day before. She could not make a cup of tea in the tiny bedsitting room as she had no kettle or cups.

She was more concerned about getting some cocaine. Would Neville bring some? Only four hours to go. She decided to leave at two to give herself plenty of time. Luckily the Escort tank had been full so there was no problem about buying petrol. She would be glad to be out of this awful room which was like a prison to her.

The owner intercepted her in the hallway. 'You settled in okay?'

'Yes thank you.'

'Only I haven't seen you bring your things in.' Had she seen the paper and recognised her? 'Bedthings and that.'

'No, they're at my friend's. I'm just going for them as a matter of fact.'

The woman, a harridan in her late fifties with battleship grey hair and chewed fingernails, peered at her suspiciously. 'That's your car in the street, isn't it?'

'The Escort.'

'Only I see there's a traffic warden stood by it.'

'Oh Christ.' She rushed to the door and stopped in horror when she opened it. The 'traffic warden' was a policeman. Was he looking for her? Had he traced her somehow from the registration number?

'This your car miss?' he called across. He looked like a member of the Politburo, hard-faced and humourless.

'Yes.' She walked over. She hated all officials. She wanted to spit on him, swear at him, cut his throat . . . throat . . .she thought of Richard and bit her lip. He was saying something about single yellow lines.

'Been here since yesterday.'

'It wouldn't start. I was changing the battery. I'm moving it now.' He was peering closely at the front of her T-shirt. Better than her face but he still made her feel sick.

'Don't park it here again.' She thrust two fingers at him as he walked away. The Escort started first time. She had decided to go through Banbury and Warwick rather than risk being spotted in Stratford, a place she never wanted to see again.

She pulled her leather jacket round her shoulders as she drove through the city centre past the Bodleian Library and the stone walled colleges. After the unlikely tropical spring fortnight, temperatures had dropped to more traditional March levels.

The roads were clear and she reached Birmingham just after five. She parked the car in the multi-storey car park next to the Albany Hotel and walked down Station Street to the back of the station. She passed the Tivoli Cinema where she had met Richard the night they fled from Stratford. None of this would have happened if she had not made that phone call.

She wondered where she would be this time tomorrow. As long as she had some cocaine she did not much care. Maybe, with Neville's money, she would get a train to London. You could hide in a big city.

She sat in the station buffet drinking a cup of tea until five to six. Buying the platform ticket left her with a penny. Down the escalator she was jostled by office, shop and business commuters homeward bound to towns like Solihull, Walsall and Bromsgrove.

Meanwhile, Erskine Porter had entered the station. . . .

Six o'clock. She had walked to the far end of the platform and back but there was no sign of Neville. She started towards 6b, the Northern continuation.

She looked up at the very moment Erskine Porter was walking down the escalator. It was the walk that alerted her, the same walk as the man she had seen outside the telephone kiosk at Temple Grafton. She stared as he came closer and when he looked up and caught her gaze, she knew she was right. She saw the flicker of recognition on his face as if he had been looking for her.

This was the man that had killed Richard. Now he was after her. Yet how did he know she would be at the station? Only Neville knew. He must be in it too. Which explained how Richard Marchant first had her number. He must have been working for Neville all the time.

His walk quickened to a run. She turned round and saw him hurrying after her. She knew now that she would have been killed at Temple Grafton if she had not hidden in the field. But would he dare attack her in front of all these passengers?

She veered to the edge of the platform to avoid a cluster of people. She heard the train approaching, an express roaring through the station at 70 m.p.h. Her feet, as she ran, were inches from the drop. He was only a few yards behind her and gaining when she stumbled and balanced precariously on the white line marking the rim of the platform.

'Steady now.' A bald man in his late thirties, not unattractive, pulled her back. 'Are you all right?'

'Yes thank you.' She swallowed breathlessly. 'I lost my footing for a second.'

'Not the best place to do it,' he remarked cheerfully. 'You were nearly under that train.'

'Yes I know. I feel a bit shaken.' A sideways glance told her that her pursuer was hovering nearby. 'I wonder, I feel a bit dizzy, could you help me to the buffet. I think I need a sit down and a cup of strong tea.'

'Why certainly.' He responded like a true hero though his physical appearance owed more to Robert Robinson than Robert Redford. 'Here, take my arm.' She leaned against him and allowed him to steer her up the escalator, a sight that attracted curious glances, a middle-aged businessman embracing a young dolly bird in leather jacket and jeans.

Ten steps behind them on the escalator was Erskine Porter, hired killer.

'Here we are, is anything the matter?' He noticed her frightened backward glances.

'Er no, I wonder. . . .' There was a row of phone booths nearby but who could she call for help? Richard was dead, Neville was the enemy. Her father? But even if she dared, what could he do? And then she thought of one person who would be on her side. Whatever the consequences of calling him, nothing could be worse than this, hunted by vicious criminals, running in constant fear of her life. 'I would like to make a phone call. Could you stay with me?'

He seemed puzzled but agreed.

'Have you got a ten pence?' She had but the one penny in all the world.

'Here you are.' He handed one over.

She took the coin and carefully dialled 01-230-1212. It was a number she remembered from being a kid, on police bulletins on the radio. Scotland Yard. She pushed in her coin as the pips went. She knew his name from the papers.

'Could I speak to Chief Inspector Knox?'

Detective Chief Inspector Glass sat at his desk at Scotland Yard, peering at the accumulated mountain of paperwork through a thick cloud of yellow smoke, the product of a day's heavy intake of Craven A. When the telephone rang it took him several seconds to locate it.

'Mr.Glass? There's a young lady on the line for Mr.Knox but he's away in Stratford. It sounds urgent. Would you take it?'

'Put her through,' said Glass. It was a respite from the paperwork. It was a wonder new recruits were not taught shorthand and typing at police college. Perhaps they were. Nothing about police college would have surprised him.

'Hello. I want to speak to Chief Inspector Knox.' She sounded young, he thought, and frightened.

'He's out, love, I'm afraid. Can I help you at all? My name's Glass.'

'Well. . . .'

'You know Robin Knox do you?'

'Sort of. . . .'

'Only I'm his father-in-law. If anything is the matter, you can tell me,' said Glass in avuncular tones. 'I know about most of his cases.' This was a lie. Even when they came to trial, Knox had to be persuaded to reveal details of his investigations.

'I'm Lynne. Richard Marchant's girl friend, you know. . . .' He certainly did know. He almost jumped to attention. His Eddie The Nose theory had come up trumps again and it was not even his case. Protocol told him he ought to put her on to Superintendent Page at the Drugs Squad but Glass had no time for protocol. '. . . the man who was murdered.'

'You're the girl who dialled 999 to say where Inspector Knox was?'

'Yes. Listen, they're after me.'

'Who?'

'This black man is following me. He killed Richard and now he's after me.'

'Where are you speaking from?'

'Birmingham.'

'Birmingham! Whereabouts?'

'On the station. He tried to push me under a train.'

'Which station?' But before she could tell him, the pips started. 'Give me your number,' shouted Glass but there was not time. The line went dead. He put the receiver down and waited. But it did not ring again.

Glass rushed into the next office and picked up a red phone. 'Glass here. I want police headquarters in Birmingham on this line, quickly. And have Sergeant Moon sent up to my office and I want a fast car ready in five minutes. And if the girl rings back for me, put it through to my extension.'

He marched resolutely back to his office, lit another Craven A and hovered· by the phone, unsuccessfully willing it to ring. Sergeant Moon walked in a minute later.

'You wanted me, sir?'

'No time to lose, lad. The car's outside.'

'What's happening?'

'We're off to Birmingham. I'll explain on the way. Hang on, the phone is ringing.' He ran next door.

'Birmingham police on the line,' said the operator. Glass explained the situation to the head of the Uniformed Branch.

'I'll get men to the station right away. I think we must assume it's New Street,' said the Midlands chief. 'I just hope we're in time.'

'I'll be with you in two hours,' promised Glass. 'Let's go Sergeant.' Moon raced behind him to the car, a Rover 800SI. 'Lucky to get one of these,' said the detective, noisily engaging first gear. 'Jump in.' He was moving away as Moon's left foot left the ground. The sergeant wished he had invested in a St. Christopher medallion. He fastened his seat belt apprehensively. Glass drove the Rover like he drove his Mini, foot flat down on the accelerator.

He had every reason to hurry. This girl was the key to the whole drugs case, she was a witness to Richard Marchant's murder and the girl who had saved the life of his daughter's husband.

By the time he arrived in Birmingham, she might be dead.

Chapter 23

'Quickly, another ten pence,' said Lynne. She turned round as the pips went but her rescuer was gone.

Instead, a black hand reached down from behind her to push the rest firmly down.

'Oh God.' She cried out in terror.

'Just walk out of the station in front of me. Don't try to get away or you'll get this in your back.' She felt a sharp point press against her spine through her leather jacket.

'No.' She lurched forward into the crowd, pushing her way to the escalator which led up to the New Street Shopping Centre. He was right behind her. She ran all the way to the top and looked wildly round for a policeman but all she could see were gangs of black youths hanging around shop doorways.

She ran past the fountain, Porter gaining with every step and then she saw two policemen at the far end of the precinct. There would be no time for explanations; one throw of Porter's knife and she would be dead.

Gasping for breath, she dashed towards them and, as she drew near, took off her right shoe and hurled it unhesitatingly through the plate glass window of Boots the Chemist.

The noise of the shattering glass startled everyone in the arcade. Erskine Porter stopped in his tracks as the two policemen jumped forward to grab her although not before her other shoe had smashed the adjoining window. He stood by helpless as she was dragged out of the precinct.

'You are under arrest,' said one of the policemen unoriginally but Lynne never heard him. Exhausted by the chase, the lack of food and the tension of the last few days, she had passed out in his arms.

Detective Chief Inspector Glass and Sergeant Moon arrived in Birmingham shortly before nine p.m., having been delayed by queues on the M1. They were greeted with the news that the girl had been picked up by the police and was now in the local hospital under surveillance.

'I'm afraid we were not able to apprehend the man following her,' apologised Superintendent Wolstenholme of the Uniformed Branch. 'In fact, my men had no idea until afterwards that she was being chased.'

'Not to worry,' sighed Glass. 'At least she is safe. When can I see her?'

'In the morning. She is suffering from exhaustion as much as anything. That and a need for some cocaine.'

'We'll come down to the station at eleven then. I assume she'll be released from the hospital.' He turned to the sergeant. 'We'd better go and find a hotel. The Midland do a nice dinner.'

The receptionist at the Midland Hotel was most apologetic. 'Only one room available for tonight I'm afraid.'

'Never mind,' said Glass. 'Mr.Moon will take that. Don't worry about me, Sergeant. I can drive over to that bed and breakfast place we stayed at in Stratford. It's only half an hour away.'

'Oh, Mrs.Marston wasn't it?'

'Lily, that's right. But I'll stay and have dinner with you first. We can put it on your bill.'

'Will you be getting in touch with Chief Inspector Knox while you're in Stratford, sir? I believe he's still there and this is his case.'

'No, I don't think so. I can sort this out for him, no sense in dragging him away from his enquiries, it might all come to nothing. Besides, I'd have no idea where to find him.'

'What about the racing case? Are we abandoning those investigations?'

'For the time being, yes. Nothing doing on that at all but never fear, something will turn up.'

In what amazing fashion Glass could never have guessed.

Refreshed after his night with the accommodating Mrs. Marston, Detective Chief Inspector Glass was in good humour for his interrogation of the girl.

Lynne sat in front of a desk in the Interview Room, still in her leather jacket, T-shirt and jeans but looking less tired than the evening before.

Glass introduced himself. 'I want you to take your time and tell me everything you know. And don't worry about Sergeant Moon. He's just here to take notes and make sure you don't try to bribe me.'

Lynne looked at him sharply, the night's sleep and the relief from the craving for cocaine having restored some of her spirit.

'Just tell me what I'm likely to get.'

'How do you mean?'

'I mean, will I go to prison?'

'That depends. What exactly have you done?'

She laughed bitterly. 'Abduction of a police officer, attempted murder - how's that for starters?'

'I thought your late friend Marchant was the abductor and murderer.'

'I was with him.'

Glass leaned across the table and looked her in the eye. 'Look, love, let's get this straight. I'm not out to nail you. I just want the man who killed Marchant and tried to kill you. And I want the names of the men involved in the drug ring. Right? Now

if I don't catch these men and we let you out of here, the odds are they'll try to kill you again. And next time they'll probably succeed.'

'You mean you'll use me as bait?'

'I mean if you tell me everything, you'll save yourself the risk.'

'God, you're a hard bugger.'

Glass looked pained. 'I don't know how bad your addiction is but I do know there are lots of other girls being persuaded to take drugs whose lives can still be saved. So I want some names. Let's start with the black fellow at the station. Have you ever seen him before?'

'Only once, the night Richard was killed. We went to a village called Temple Grafton near Stratford. Richard had to meet somebody there. I waited in the car and I saw this man follow him. I drove away.'

'And Richard was murdered?'

'Yes.'

'You knew Marchant was a pusher. Who did he work for?'

'A man called Taylor. I never saw him. Richard used to talk to him on the telephone. I have no idea where he lived.'

'How did you meet Marchant?'

'He used to go around with this crowd of people.'

'And he got you onto drugs?'

'No, I was already on them.' She stopped. Should she tell him about Neville? She was only guessing that he had told the black man she was waiting at the station. What if that had been a coincidence? Neville might have been waiting at the other end of the platform. But she did not really believe that. Glass was looking at her enquiringly.

'There is one thing you ought to know. A man I used to go out with. He was the one who got me onto coke. Well, I rang him yesterday asking for his help, money to get away.'

'And?'

'It was he who told me to go to New Street Station at 6 o'clock.'

'And nobody else knew?'

'No. But it is probably just coincidence.'

'I don't believe in those,' said Glass. 'What was his name?'

She took a deep breath. 'Lord Crossens. You may have heard of him.'

Glass stared at her incredulously. 'The racehorse owner?'

'That's the one.'

'Did you not know that he owned the house that you and Marchant lived in in Stratford?'

It was her turn to look surprised. 'No.' It was all beginning to fit in. It *must* have been from Neville that Richard first got her number.

'Until yesterday, had you any idea Lord Crossens might have been involved?'

'None at all. Richard never spoke about him. He knew I used to go out with him but that's all.'

'How did you come to go out with him? A bit old for you I would have thought.' Glass himself preferred women approaching pensionable age.

'Part of the attraction, I guess. I was straight out of school and he took me to all these fabulous parties.'

'What about his wife?'

'He wasn't married then, at least, not to her. He married her when his divorce came through, which is when I got the Big E.'

'By which time he had you hooked on drugs?'

'Yes. Then Richard phoned me. I suppose he must have got my number from Neville though I didn't realise it at the time. Anyway, I started going out with him.'

'You knew then he was pushing drugs?'

'Of course. Where do you think I got mine?' Her eyes flamed for a second. 'I'm sorry.'

'That's all right. Would you like a cup of tea?' She nodded. 'Sergeant, order us a large pot.' He took out his packet of Craven A and offered her one. 'It's the nearest thing to hard drugs they let you smoke in this country.' She took one and allowed him to light it. 'So, you then went to live with Marchant?'

'After a few weeks, yes.'

'What did your parents have to say about that?'

'My mother is dead. I had had rows with Daddy about Neville, him being so much older, and then about the drugs. He knew I was taking them. He found some in my room. When I went to live with Richard, he told me never to come back.'

'And you haven't seen him since?'

'Once, a few weeks before Christmas when I was out shopping. We didn't speak.'

'I see.' Glass blew out a cloud of empyreumatic smoke. On the evidence there was nothing he could pin on Lord Crossens, Taylor was a complete mystery figure and Marchant was dead. He was not getting very far. 'What about the night Chief Inspector Knox was kidnapped? Did Marchant do that alone?'

'No. He hired two heavies from the local Rent-a-Mob. Nobody he knew.'

'How did he find out Knox was a detective?'

'Believe it or not, that was your fault. I saw him talking to you that day in the Stratford Moat House and I thought you looked like a pi - er policeman.'

'Oh.' Glass was disconsolate. He had always cherished the notion that he might be mistaken for an actor or a retired football hero.

'Anyway, I hung around the bar after he had gone and I heard you talking to this grey haired bloke about dope.'

That must have been Jeffrey Leek-Turner. Glass smiled to himself at the irony of it. 'I was actually discussing doping,' he said. 'I was working on this case about racing fraud. Incidentally, that involved Lord Crossens too. Someone was stopping his horses from winning.'

She laughed. 'Probably my daddy, he hated him enough.'

Glass looked at her strangely. 'Funny you should say that. I asked Lord Crossens if he had any enemies.'

'And what did he say?'

'He said they would not have the guts to do anything about it. What does your father do, Lynne? By the way, I don't know what the Lynne stands for. Is it your full Christian name?'

'You can't have read the report sheet,' retorted the girl. 'My full name is Belinda, Belinda Bellis. My father is the racing trainer.'

'Christ Almighty,' he gasped. 'It all falls into place. Don Bellis.'

'You know my father?'

'I spoke to him only a fortnight ago. One of his horses fell in the Cheltenham Gold Cup and the jockey was killed.'

'I read about it; Thom Snaipe. But I don't get the connection with Neville.'

Glass's mind ticked away. Bellis must have drugged Willie Leigh and warned off John Haile. Then, when the Jockey Club investigator started asking questions, he fixed one of his own runners to divert suspicion from both himself and from Lord Crossens as the only targets. But it all went tragically wrong.

'A red herring,' he said aloud. 'Ah, here is the tea. I think we might go along and visit your father later, Lynne; a family reunion. Will you be mother, Sergeant?'

So, he had one case sewn up. What about the other? He still had no evidence that would convict Crossens or Taylor.

'Did Marchant never keep records of his transactions?'

'Never. He was very careful.'

'What about address books?'

'Didn't you find them in the house?'

Here Glass was stumped. Robin Knox had been dealing with the case but he was sure if anything had been found Taylor and Crossens would have been arrested. 'No. Only enough drugs to put the occupiers away for a long time.'

Belinda Bellis put down her cup. 'Do you intend charging me with possessing drugs, Chief Inspector? Only, I just might be able to help you.' She looked him directly in the face.

Glass knew a trade-in when he saw one. He glanced up at Sergeant Moon who was staring hard at the ceiling. 'No drugs were found on you,' he said carefully. 'Which is not to say they might not be later.' The message was plain.

'You surely don't mean you would manufacture evidence? Not a policeman?'

'It has been known,' said Glass. 'Juries never seem able to comprehend that half the policemen in witness boxes are lying through their teeth.'

'You admit that?'

'Not in public and Sergeant Moon is stone deaf. We have to get our convictions somehow.' He smiled benignly. 'Do we have a deal?'

'We have a deal. I know where Richard's address book might be.'

'Where?'

'In the house, in a secret hiding place, I can show you.'

'Finish your tea and we'll go there. Sergeant Moon, arrange for the car and tell Stratford police to get hold of Chief Inspector Knox. Tell him to meet us at the house.'

'I thought you didn't know where he was.' Moon learned more about official chicanery every day he spent in the Force.

'That was yesterday.' He turned to the girl. 'He'll be able to thank you for saving his life. Then, after that, we'll go to your father's.'

'He won't be in. I've just thought, tomorrow is the Grand National. He'll be on his way to Aintree.'

'The Grand National,' echoed Glass. 'So it is, I'd forgotten. Oh good, I fancy another day at the races and I've got a few quid on Sailor's Delight, even with that berk riding . . .' He stopped. Lord Crossens riding Sailor's Delight and his life's ambition was to win the Grand National. Would Don Bellis dare risk another 'accident' at Aintree?

'Come on,' he said. 'I need to be at Aintree by tomorrow morning but first we must go to Stratford. I hope, Lynne, that you are not a nervous passenger.' Sergeant Moon groaned.

Chapter 24

The cream of the town's business and professional men at the Rotary Club dinner applauded warmly as their chairman sat down. He had just announced another substantial sum raised for Cancer Research, not a small percentage of which was his own personal contribution, a fact he was careful to mention in his speech.

'Well done, Bernard,' whispered a dyspeptic individual to his left. Bernard smiled and poured himself another glass of finest vintage claret. The man was a J.P., a person of influence and worth cultivating.

Bernard Taylor played golf once a week with the editor of the local newspaper and consequently his photograph appeared regularly in the gossip pages showing him giving support to local causes. His bridge evenings with the bank manager and his lady wife meant he had an unlimited overdraft and the fact that he never got stopped for speeding in his Rolls Royce with the personalised number plate might have been attributable to the evenings spent with the Chief Constable at his club.

Nobody knew the exact nature of Taylor's business. When asked, he mentioned vaguely the import and export trade and left it to people to supply their own interpretation. In a society where esteem was measured by the amount of money given to The Donkey Sanctuary or Oxfam he was well respected.

'Staying for a jar, Bernard?' asked the leader of the Chamber of Commerce.

'No thanks, Harvey. I must be in by eleven tonight or the little woman will give me what for.'

The 'little woman' (Agnes, solicitor's daughter, mother of his two children away at boarding school) was usually in bed when he returned but tonight, as he swung the Rolls into the gateway, he observed that all the lights in the house were on. Puzzled, he walked round from the garage, passing two strange Sierras in his front drive, and inserted his key in the lock.

The big shock came when he pushed open the front door. Five armed police officers stood in a semi-circle facing him. Automatically he stepped back but two more men had emerged from the shadows behind him.

'Bernard Taylor. I'm Detective Chief Inspector Knox from New Scotland Yard. I've just searched your house and have a warrant for your arrest.'

'What now?' said Robin Knox to Detective Chief Inspector Glass. It was 1 a.m. and they were back at the West Midlands Police H.Q. in Birmingham having left Lynne at a hotel in Stratford in the care of Sergeant Moon. Taylor was in custody being photographed, fingerprinted and documented.

'Nothing tonight, it's too late. Tomorrow I'll go up to Liverpool and collect Lord Crossens for you.' He grinned wickedly. 'Did you ever finish dredging the river by the way?'

'Very funny,' said Knox. 'Remember, you've got nothing on Crossens yet and you won't have unless Taylor talks and we've only got him on possession so far.'

'Very careless of him leaving that heroin behind the chimney. His wife got a bit upset when you started stripping the wallpaper where the dogs were sniffing.'

'He's getting a bit upset too. He's howling for his brief and I don't think we can put him off too much longer.'

'Let him howl. So long as no word gets out until I've arrested Crossens. You got somebody to stay at Taylor's house, keep an eye on his wife?'

'Yes. And the telephone has been accidentally disconnected. I hope nothing goes wrong.'

'It won't, don't worry. Wait until we get hold of the rest of the people in the address book, you'll hear more squeaks than in one of Denis Healey's lemons. I see your friend Lucerelli's name is in there.'

'So is mine, as Jeremy Rowlands. We are both care of Lyn at Trolfid Records, the girl who left to have a baby.'

Glass flicked through the pages. 'He did well out of the pop world. This could be the biggest drugs clean-up since Operation Julie.'

'I wish I shared your confidence. I should have rung Superintendent Page at the Drugs Squad by rights.'

'Why? We're going all right on our own. We'll only arouse suspicion if we bring half the Met up here. We'll have the two ringleaders by tomorrow night, what more could he want?'

'I want them on a murder rap,' said Knox quietly.

'So you will as soon as we find this black man. He'll be our hit man. Once he realises we've got the men who gave him his orders he'll soon cough.'

'We have to find him first.'

'Taylor will tell us.'

'No way.'

'Just give me twenty minutes alone with him, Robin. I'll get you the name you want.' He held up his hand as the other was about to protest. 'No questions.' Knox reluctantly stepped aside and Glass marched down to the cells.

'Good morning, Mr.Taylor. I am Detective Chief Inspector Glass.'

'Now you listen to me . . .'

'No, you listen to me, Mr.Taylor. It is past midnight and I don't like missing my sleep. I have a few things to say to you to put you in the picture regarding your position. First of all, you can kiss goodbye forever to your pillar of the community act.

We have already got you for possession of heroin and by this time tomorrow we will have you for distributing, importing, selling - the lot. A good twenty-five years there, I reckon.'

'Just try it.'

'Oh we will, you see, we have Marchant's address book. Silly of him to keep records, wasn't it? Lord Crossens will be joining you behind bars shortly and I don't need to tell you that a man with his power and money is going to try and save his own skin at the expense of others.'

'If you've got it all so neatly tied up, what do you want from me?'

'Right now, I want the name of the man you hired to kill Richard Marchant.'

'I know nothing about that.'

Glass ignored him. 'It appears that the eye-witness has poor eyesight and finds it difficult to distinguish between a coloured man and a suntanned one. I have just shown her the photographs we have taken of yourself and she is willing to swear that you were at Temple Grafton the night Richard Marchant was killed. Where were you at six o'clock that evening Mr.Taylor?'

'You must be joking. I've killed nobody.' He thought. Six o'clock. He was with his mistress at the apartment he had set up for her, not something he wanted to disclose.

'This same eye-witness swears you were at New Street Station, following her with a knife in your hand. This knife.' Glass flashed a steel blade past Taylor's eyes, too quickly for him to see that it had come from the station canteen. 'Found in your pockets when searched. The knife that murdered Richard Marchant.'

Taylor was silent. For him the drug trafficking had been a business, albeit a highly illegal one. When he had needed to use violence, he had simply picked up a phone and paid somebody else to carry out his instructions. This was the first time the hard reality of the criminal world had reached him.

'The name and address,' repeated Glass. 'Now.'

'I - er don't know his address. I only have a telephone number. I only told him to frighten Marchant, not to kill him, honestly. It was Crossens's idea.'

'Save your whining for the judge.' Glass took down the number and went back to Knox.

'The man you want,' he said cheerfully, 'is Erskine Porter. O.K.?'

Knox regarded him warily. 'Is Taylor unmarked?'

'Good heavens, yes,' protested Glass piously. 'You didn't think I'd touched him did you? Anyway, he's ready to make a statement now.' He looked up at the clock above the door. 'Time I was getting to bed. I have to drive back to Stratford yet.'

'I wish I could join you,' said Knox, 'but some of us have work to do.'

'When you get to my age,' Glass said, 'you need your sleep.'

'Rubbish. Everyone knows you're still on your feet and drinking long after everyone else has passed out exhausted. Where are you staying?'

'Oh, just a little bed and breakfast place. Quite comfortable.'

'Are you sure you don't want me to go to Aintree with you tomorrow?'

'Quite sure. You look after Taylor and Sergeant Moon and I'll bring Lord Crossens back with us. Besides, I have a little business of my own up there which I want to clear up.'

Glass was wondering how Belinda Bellis would react if, after reuniting her with her father, he arrested Don Bellis for murder.

Chapter 25

Detective Chief Inspector Glass emerged from Mrs. Marston's love-nest at nine o'clock and drove to the Arden Hotel opposite the theatre where Lynne and Sergeant Moon were waiting for him in reception.

'My, a big difference,' he said, commenting on the new cotton dress the girl wore in place of the grubby T-shirt and jeans which had adorned her body for the past fortnight. He did not publicise the fact that it was he who had provided the money to buy it, albeit out of expenses. 'It's a wonder Sergeant Moon didn't leap on you in the night.' Moon blushed and the inspector thought it unlikely that he would leap on anybody, least of all Ethel, his affianced.

They all climbed into the Rover, Glass helping Lynne into the front seat. 'Are you nervous?' he asked.

Lynne nodded. 'He might not want to see me.'

'I think he will.'

The journey to Aintree took longer than expected when the car broke down near Stoke, leaving them stranded on the hard shoulder of the M6 for two hours, waiting for the A.A. 'No wonder people buy Japanese cars,' grumbled Glass. 'I'm writing to British Leyland about this.'

The mechanic took a further twenty minutes to rectify the fault and Glass roared away at 110 m.p.h., the speed he maintained until he came off the M57 at Maghull, a couple of miles from the racecourse.

Even so, the second race of the afternoon was about to start when they entered the grounds. Glass made straight for the course officials to whom he explained his mission. Mention of Jeffrey Leek-

Turner's name sealed their co-operation and an office was made available to him.

'You stay here with Sergeant Moon,' he told Lynne. 'I want to speak to your father alone first.'

Despite the excellent TV coverage the Grand National still attracted a huge number of spectators who felt that the tremendous atmosphere of the occasion more than compensated for the small portion of the race they would actually see. Glass had some difficulty reaching Don Bellis whom he eventually found beside his horsebox saddling Reverend Shaker. 'Can you spare a moment, Mr.Bellis?' asked the detective. The trainer recognised him and gave the head lad instructions to walk the horse down to the paddock.

'More trouble, Inspector?'

'Chief Inspector,' corrected Glass, 'and, yes, more trouble. For you, that is.'

'What do you mean?'

'Just that I KNOW, Mr.Bellis. I know that you made the phone call to John Haile, I know that you drugged Willie Leigh and Thom Snaipe, I even know where you got the dope. And,' he paused theatrically for maximum effect, 'I know all about Belinda. In fact, she is here today with my Sergeant.'

Not a muscle of Don Bellis's face moved yet in an instant he had aged ten years.

'Does she know?'

'About you? No.'

'How did you find out?'

'Coincidence really. I met your daughter on another case, a drugs case. I'm surprised you didn't see her picture in the papers.'

'I only read the racing pages. You can't alter the news so reading about it won't make it any better.'

'Anyway, she told me about her association with Lord Crossens which ended up with her a junkie and leaving the happy family home. And suddenly I had my missing motive - a man who had every reason to hate Lord Crossens.'

'But one of my horses was got at, you know that?' His protest came too late.

'To put me off the scent, the oldest trick in the book.' Glass wished he had spotted it before. 'Pity that young jockey had to die because that makes it murder of course.' His tone remained conversational but the trainer recoiled as if a bomb had been dropped.

'But it was an accident, you know it was.'

'If you had not doped him he would not have died. To a simple man like myself, that's murder.'

'What will I get?' Bellis looked a beaten man.

'Who knows? Ten years? Hard to tell these days.' With the benevolent attitude of modern courts, Glass would not have been surprised at a £20 fine and Thom Snaipe's parents would thereupon have felt justified in employing Erskine Porter's services but, being a policeman, he did not say so.

'I only did it for Belinda. I loved her. She was our only child, our baby.' Another one going to cry, thought Glass. Why did he have this effect on people when he questioned them? 'I meant no harm to anyone but him.'

'Why didn't you go round and kick his head in then, like anyone else would have done? Like he deserved. And why wait till she'd been gone over a year?'

'I saw her in town one day, shopping. She has never even spoken to me - her Dad. Her eyes looked sort of vacant. It set it all off again - the hatred.'

'The next day was the Hennessy Gold Cup. Crossens was on TV saying he was going to win the race and I thought not if I can help it, you bastard. Belinda had left some of her tablets in the house when she left. I never touched her room you know, just in case she came back.' The tears welled again like Roman springs in Bellis's eyes. 'Anyway, I thought if I slipped one of those sugar lumps in the jockey's tea he might get a bit dizzy, have a bad ride.'

'But he fell, nearly got killed, broke several major bones and could not ride for weeks which meant severe hardship for his family.'

'At least Crossens did not win the race.'

'And that justifies it does it?' stormed Glass, angry now. 'That justifies frightening the life out of a sensitive young jockey who had done you no harm whatsoever? You won't get ten years Bellis, you'll be put in Broadmoor. You're insane.'

'No, no. I didn't mean to hurt them.' Then his whine changed to a triumphant snarl. 'I've got him this time though.'

'What do you mean by that?' Glass felt his skin go clammy. He shook the trainer's shoulder vigorously.

'He's riding Sailor's Delight in the National. Well, he won't get very far. Not without his bridle.'

'What have you done, man?' Glass lashed the trainer's face with the back of his hand.

Don Bellis laughed. 'Just cut it, that's all. And stuck it together with glue, but it won't hold out for long. I don't give much for his chances at Becher's. Let's hope there are a good few horses coming up behind to stamp on his head.'

'You fool,' cried Glass. 'I must get to the starting post before it's too late. You may be killing another innocent man, Bellis. Willie Leigh is riding Sailor's Delight.'

Albert Beaton was talking to his daughter in the paddock when Glass ran up, puffing noisily, his cheeks redder than a vampire's gums. 'Hey Walter, you're not chasing Steve Ovett are you?'

'Willie, has he left yet?' panted the detective.

'Yes, he's gone down for the parade,' replied Nicola. She looked at him in alarm. 'Is something the matter?'

'His bridle, it's been cut. We must stop him.'

'Oh God.'

'It was Don Bellis, he thought Lord Crossens was riding.'

'I talked him out of it,' said Bertie, 'it's my fault. But why Bellis?'

'No time to explain. We must catch Willie before it's too late.'

Nicola was already on her way. 'For God's sake, hurry,' she screamed. 'The parade's nearly over, they'll be going down to the start any minute.' She pushed her way through the crowds, her father and Glass behind her. 'If we don't get there, Willie will be killed.'

The biggest cheer of the afternoon heralded the arrival of Red Rum, three times winner of the Grand National, to lead the parade of horses past the grandstand.

His sleek, bay coat shone magnificently, he wore his familiar white sheepskin noseband and he looked far more likely to win the race than any of the horses actually entered.

By contrast the diminutive Sailor's Delight, with Willie Leigh confidently astride him, looked little more than a pony against Red Rum's 16.2 hands. Yet, like the big horse, he had the power and the will to win and, like Red Rum too, he loved the crowds

They walked past the stands then cantered out to the first fence to get the feel of the turf and allow the horses a glimpse of the obstacles in store for them. Then they made their way towards the starting line at the end of the stands.

'They're coming under starter's orders.' The voice of the course commentator echoed from the tannoy.

A hundred yards from the start Detective Chief Inspector Glass, Albert Beaton and Nicola Beaton were valiantly trying to force their way through the crowds.

They never made it.

The flag went down and the horses shot forward as one. The Grand National Steeplechase (Handicap), the world's most celebrated horse race, was under way.

Chapter 26

Sailor's Delight was in the middle of the pack as they raced towards the first fence, cheered on by hundreds of spectators lining the popular side where flags of every nation flew. The gelding was favourite at 7-1 but the odds would have been drastically lengthened had the real handicap been known - that Willie Leigh was facing the world's toughest fences with a broken bridle.

The biggest crowd out on the course was at the sixth fence, the legendary Becher's Brook. Despite the sunshine, the going was heavy after two days of rain in the North West and seven horses had already fallen at the first five fences. Sailor's Delight was in the leading pack as they jumped Becher's where another three horses fell. As they neared the Canal Turn, he was lying ninth.

'I'm going to fetch Sergeant Moon,' said Glass. 'I'll see you in the stands. I take it you'll be watching the race.'

'We can't see much of it,' said Nikki, 'but I don't think I want to.'

'How dangerous is it?' Glass asked Bertie.

'It isn't insurmountable. Fred Winter won the French Grand National in 1962 on Mandarin with a broken bridle. In fact he rode over half the race with it but he was an exceptional jockey and the fences at Auteuil are nowhere near as severe as the fences at Aintree.'

'You see,' explained Nikki, 'you can't stop or steer the horse without a bridle. The horse will therefore tend to run away with the jockey and with no bit to guide him at the fences. . . .' She started to cry, unusually for her.

Glass went to the offices and brought Sergeant Moon and Belinda Bellis out in time to see the runners pass the stand for the first time, the black gelding going well, still in ninth place.

At the West Midlands Police Headquarters in Birmingham Detective Chief Inspector Knox was listening to the race on the radio.

'And they're coming up to Becher's for the second time,' cried the Irish voice of Michael O'Hehir, 'and it's still Hush in the lead followed by Woodhey Vickers and Son of J.R. neck and neck a length behind, then Mister Charles, Bubble and Squeak, Sailor's Delight and Crikey Moses with Reverend Shaker and Oscar a length behind them.'

A loose horse was also in the pack as Willie Leigh steadied his mount for the big jump. As Sailor's Delight was about to take off, the loose horse veered in front of them. Willie pulled the reins sharply to steer his horse clear.

Which was the moment when the bridle broke.

The reins came loose in his hands, the fence was upon them, the jockey helpless, but Sailor's Delight took off magnificently and cleared Becher's with a tremendous leap. Willie held on, using his body to steer the animal as they made the left hand turn.

Should he stop and dismount or should he go on and risk injury with his chance of winning virtually gone? He would need all his strength and skill just to stay on board. But he reckoned without the almost supernatural understanding of Sailor's Delight.

They jumped two fences without mishap and came into the Canal Turn towards Valentine's Brook.

Hush was now a good three lengths clear but the pace was too fast for him, he was going flat out too soon. At Valentine's he stumbled from exhaustion and had to be pulled up.

Five fences to go and, incredibly, Sailor's Delight increased his speed. His ears were pricked and he responded to the urgent movements of his jockey's body. He overtook Bubble and Squeak and Mister Charles.

Now they were in third place but every jump seemed twice the normal height. Willie hung on, tiring, his body aching as he used all his strength to guide the little black gelding. He was glad he was not riding a bigger horse.

Two more fences, Sailor's Delight galloped on. They came alongside Son of J.R. whose jockey looked across as they ran neck and neck and stared incredulously at Willie Leigh's useless bridle. Willie gritted his teeth and held on.

They jumped the next fence still level. Now only two to go and Sailor's Delight started to move away from Son of J.R. He was only two lengths behind the leader. Behind him Crikey Moses was making a late run.

The penultimate fence and the fading Mister Charles fell. Only one left.

Willie Leigh held his breath as they came over the last fence. Up jumped Sailor's Delight and they were over. Now, could they hold on? They came up to the elbow, one furlong to go on the run in, but Willie remembered how Devon Loch had stumbled in 1956 when fifty yards from the finishing post, depositing Dick Francis on the grass and depriving him of certain victory. And he had not had a broken bridle. Willie thought there must be a fair chance of him repeating the tragedy.

He looked round. Crikey Moses was closing in on him but Son of J.R. was fighting back. They were only a length behind.

And then, Sailor's Delight surged suddenly forward like a sports car slipping into overdrive and all at once Willie forgot about falling or the broken bridle or the horses behind him and looked instead to the one horse in front. He wanted to WIN this Grand National.

'And now the favourite, Sailor's Delight, is positively storming up the straight, I don't think I have ever seen a horse finish so fast in the Grand National and there is no way that Woodhey Vickers is going to hold his lead. Sailor's Delight flashes past him, ears pricked, obviously enjoying every minute of a tremendous victory against all odds and the most popular winner here at Aintree since Aldaniti in 1982 and he crosses the line in just nine minutes and twenty seconds, a new record and Crikey Moses and Son of J.R. come in second and third.'

Nicola Beaton and her father danced around hugging one another in the stands, Glass waved his brown trilby in the air and even Belinda Bellis and Sergeant Moon were cheering, intoxicated by the euphoria of the moment.

'He's done it, Willie's done it,' screamed Nikki in delight.

'He's won the bloody National,' laughed Glass, mentally calculating his winnings.

'Come on, let's get down to the Winner's Enclosure,' said Bertie and Glass saw Lynne hang back.

'I don't want to see Neville, not when you arrest him.'

'Arrest?' said Bertie. 'What's all this?' Glass explained briefly as they walked.

'Lord Crossens running a drug ring? I don't believe it,' said Bertie.

'It's true,' said Glass. 'More money in cocaine than in jam.'

'So all these accidents were to get back at him?'

Lynne looked sharply at Glass. 'What accidents?'

'I'm sorry, love, but you'll have to know.' He told her about Don Bellis. 'He did it for you really.'

'Where is he now? I must go to him.'

'With his horses I suppose.' Reverend Shaker had fallen at The Chair.

'So when are you arresting Lord Crossens?' asked Nicola as Lynne went in search of her father. 'And what is going to happen to Don Bellis?'

'He'll probably go to jail but at least he's got his daughter back which will be more than enough compensation. As for Lord Crossens, I'll wait till all this is over and he's got his trophy from the Queen, then I'll have him.'

'You'll have to be quick then,' said Nikki. 'He's leaving for Buenos Aires after the presentation.'

'What? How do you know that? Is that right?' He turned to Bertie.

'His helicopter is waiting out there on the course.'

'Come on Sergeant,' said Glass urgently, 'we'll get him now.' He thought of the other girls like Belinda Bellis, whose lives had been ruined by drugs, and of his son-in-law hanging in that summer house. 'Ruin his moment of glory.'

'His life's ambition, you know,' said Bertie. 'I never liked the man but I must admit I'm glad his horse won.'

They arrived at the Winner's Enclosure just as Willie Leigh was riding Sailor's Delight in. Bertie Beaton went across to take the reins, TV and press cameramen clustered round, holding microphones out, Lord Crossens and his wife appeared and all around the crowd cheered, held in by a cordon of police. Nicola took the blanket from the head lad to put round the steaming horse as Willie dismounted to be weighed. The Queen gathered the trophy ready for the presentation but the owner was destined never to receive it.

Into this maelstrom of excitement stepped the stern figure of Detective Chief Inspector Glass. Watched by millions of television viewers all over the world, he pushed past reporters and cameramen, took out his handcuffs and said in a voice audible to every nearby microphone, 'Lord Crossens, I am Detective Chief Inspector Glass of the Metropolitan Police and I have a warrant here for your arrest on a charge of murdering Richard Marchant . . .'

He got no further. Crossens swung a right hook which sent him sprawling. Sergeant Moon moved forward but the earl threw a sharp left uppercut which caught him on the point of the jaw and he went crashing to the ground.

'Get off that horse.' Crossens grabbed Willie Leigh's leg as he was dismounting, pulled him to the

222

grass, snatched his whip out of his hand and clambered into the saddle himself. 'Move!' he shouted at the horse, kicking it in the side and brandishing the whip. And the crowd scattered as the owner rode his Grand National winner towards the course.

Police, reporters, cameramen and spectators followed them as they jumped the barrier and headed towards the waiting helicopter. Two police horses set off in pursuit but Lord Crossens had a good start. In the stands the crowd could scarcely believe what was happening. Neither could Lady Crossens.

The blades were already rotating as they came closer to the machine, Lord Crossens swinging the whip cruelly about the head of the tired horse. 'Get this bleddy thing off the ground,' he shouted at the pilot as he scrambled from the saddle, stooping to avoid the slipstream and pushing the horse aside as he did so.

In that moment he sealed his fate.

Sailor's Delight, Racehorse of the Year, lashed out with his back leg and his steel horseshoe caught his owner squarely in the groin, puncturing his left testicle. Crossens slumped in agony to the ground and when the first of the mounted policemen arrived, he was unconscious. The drama was over.

In a press conference shown live on TV later in the afternoon, Detective Chief Inspector Glass described Crossens as a 'vicious criminal who brought suffering, degradation and death to hundreds of innocent people' and claimed full credit for his arrest and the break-up of the drug ring.

Lord Crossens himself lay in nearby Walton Hospital where surgeons were forced to remove both testicles because of what one doctor referred to as the 'billiard ball effect'.

Nicola Beaton was amused when she heard the news. 'So he's a gelding now,' she smiled sweetly. 'How appropriate.'

In the evening they attended a celebration dinner at Liverpool's Adelphi Hotel, Glass looking strangely distinguished in evening dress lent to him by Bertie Beaton, a man of similarly rotund dimensions. Willie Leigh announced his retirement from riding and Bertie disclosed he was to join him as his partner in the stables.

Glass telephoned his son-in-law from the hotel. 'I'm sorry I couldn't get down tonight,' he said. Knox listened to the noise of the festivities in the background and said nothing.

'I'll take Taylor down to London then,' he said bitterly. All his work on the Shula Sun tour and his ordeal in the summerhouse seemed to have been for nothing. Once again, Glass had grabbed all the glory. 'Don't worry about me. You have a good time. What about Bellis?'

'He won't run away,' said Glass. 'I must be getting back. We're having the toast any minute.'

'Hard luck about Crossens.'

'His own fault,' replied the Chief Inspector. 'His own animal and he did not know the first rule of the stables. You never walk behind a horse.'

And Glass returned to the champagne.

THE END